Mike Faricy

Mr. Swirlee

(Originally published as Mr. Softee)

Mr. Swirlee
ISBN-13: 978-1493607440
ISBN-10: 1493607448
ASIN: B0056396DS

To Teresa

"The pretty girl took the soldier's hand, and for the first time, in a very, very long time, he felt safe."

Mr. Swirlee

Chapter One

"What did they do?" Mr. Swirlee screamed, his bald head immediately went from beet red to dark purple. "You idiot. Did you hear anything I said? They tried to kill me for God's sake."

His real name was Weldon Swirlmann. Although he insisted I call him Mr. Swirlee. Screaming made him even more red-faced than normal. His crimson face was propped up on the pile of starched white hospital pillows. Blips on the monitor screens arraigned alongside his bed jumped accordingly with every outburst.

"I'm telling ya, they wanted to murder me. Only those brats showing up on their bikes stopped things from getting any worse."

"What did the police say?" I asked.

"The cops, you gotta be kidding. You think I trust them? They were probably in on the deal, the bastards," he screamed.

Beep, beep, beep, beep, beep. One of the monitors had now switched to alarm mode.

"Oh, these goddamned things." He reached up to yank the cord out of the monitor.

The young woman introduced to me as Lola sat up just a little straighter in the vinyl visitor's chair near the end of his bed. Using my acquired skills as a private investigator I deduced she was Mr. Swirlee's daughter. She adjusted her blouse with both hands, pinched the cream-colored silk between thumb and forefinger just above her belt line then tugged.

Each one of her elegant, long red nails sported a delicate little gold design, and she seemed to function effortlessly despite the long-nail handicap. The tug exposed another inch or two of deep cleavage. She was beautiful, in a sort of peroxide way.

For the first time in twenty minutes she spoke, cautioning Mr. Swirlee in an exceptionally high, squeaky, little-girl voice.

"Careful, precious, remember what Doctor…"

"That quack? He should just stick to his job, which is getting me the hell out of here. Damn it, Haskins, they tried to kill me."

"Actually, it's Haskell, Devlin Haskell."

Mr. Swirlee glared at me for a couple of long seconds.

"Whatever. The bastards tried to kill me. They couldn't buy me out, couldn't run me out, so now they finally tried to kill me."

"Who's they?" I asked.

"What in the hell am I paying you for? That's what I want you to find out. You're supposed to tell me just who in the hell did this." With a wave of his hands Mr. Swirlee indicated the bandages wrapped around his left leg and propped up on a series of pillows.

"Actually, Sir, no offense, but you aren't paying me. At least you haven't yet. The first I heard of this was the message from your…from Lola last night." I

5

nodded at the smiling Barbie doll sitting up straight in the vinyl chair.

She winked back slowly and licked her lower lip.

My heart skipped a beat and I quickly refocused on Mr. Swirlee. "So anyway, you haven't paid me. Not that that's the point. What makes you think this was intentional? I mean your car was…."

"Car? That wasn't just a car. That was a Mercedes CL 600. Know what they go for, Haskins?"

"Haskell."

"They start at about one twenty. Damn it, grounds right there to shoot the bastards."

"But what makes you so sure it wasn't some idiot involved in a simple hit and run?" I asked.

"Simple! Does this look simple to you? I got a damn business to run. Think I can do that while I'm stuck in this nut house? Simple, he says, Jesus, I ought to…"

"Thank you, Mr. Haskell, we'll be in touch," Lola squeaked in her cartoon voice then slinked to her feet. With the six-inch stiletto heels she stood about five foot eight. Her skirt was just a little longer than the black belt with the rhinestone buckle wrapped around her slim waist. She extended her right hand. When I took it she rubbed the back of my hand with her left, then raised an eyebrow and flashed a lustful smirk.

Or was I just imagining that?

Mr. Swirlee looked out the window, unaware. His monitors had returned to a normal pattern.

"Let me see about clearing my calendar and I'll get back to you tomorrow."

"We look forward to it." Lola smiled, still rubbing the back of my hand, in no apparent hurry to let go. She suddenly tickled the palm of my hand with her finger.

6

"Just find out who in the hell did this." Mr. Swirlee grumbled from his bed then turned back to the window, clenching and unclenching his jaw.

Chapter Two

I didn't really have a calendar, let alone one to clear. I dropped by The Spot bar, just to see if anyone was looking for me. No one was.

Mr. Swirlee ruled an empire of ice cream trucks. A fleet of pink-and-blue trucks every parent in the seven-county metro area had come to despise. The trucks crawled through neighborhood streets, playing a chimed version of "Oh where, oh where has my little dog gone?" until you wanted to scream.

Children ran back into their homes, begging for two or three dollars for one of Mr. Swirlee's overpriced ice cream treats. Frankly, there was a part of me that was more than a little amazed some crazed father hadn't tried to kill Mr. Swirlee long before now. I decided to do some checking.

"Economic development," the voice cooed into the phone.

"Connie Ortiz, please," I rasped back, hoping I'd disguised my voice.

"Who may I say is calling, please?" You could almost hear the frost forming on the words. I knew it wasn't going to work, but I foolishly tried anyway.

"I'm calling on behalf of Haskell Investigations," I said.

"And your name?" she asked, a chilling accusation in her voice.

"Devlin Haskell," I said grimacing, waiting for the expected blast. I wasn't disappointed.

"Oh, I didn't recognize your voice at first. Something more than a cold? Hopefully."

"Is this Sandy?" I asked, hoping to charm my way past the minefield.

"Who exactly did you expect to be answering the phone?"

"I…I wasn't sure. I thought it might be you, Sandy, but I really didn't recognize your voice. It's been awhile, you know?"

"Mmm-mmm, not long enough. Let me see if she can take your call. Hold please."

I knew the drill, I'd be on hold for three to five minutes, and Connie Ortiz would be unable to take my call. The truth was Sandy wouldn't even try. Still upset about a minor fender bender I had driving her car a couple of years ago.

We had been heading to my place. Sandy was way too over-served to drive, so I thought I'd help. Under the circumstances, it had seemed like a good idea at the time to just walk away from the accident scene. At three in the morning we quietly staggered away from what was left of the parked car and Sandy's damaged Toyota. No good deed goes unpunished.

"I'm sorry, she must have stepped out. May I take a message and have her return your call?"

Why bother? It's the same every time I call. I knew Sandy never tried to reach Connie Ortiz. If I leave a message, Sandy won't deliver it. It served me right for calling Sandy's PMS hotline.

"Okay, thanks for trying Sandy. If you could have her call me? She's got my number. Great to..."

Sandy abruptly hung up. I'd have to reach Connie at home later tonight.

"You want another one, Dev?" Jimmy, bartender extraordinaire, nodded toward my empty Leinenkugel's glass.

"Thanks Jimmy, but I better not. I've got a pretty busy day," I lied.

"Really? You got some business?" Jimmy sounded genuinely surprised.

"Yeah, checking a few things out for Mr. Swirlee. It shouldn't take..."

"That ice cream guy?"

"Yeah, that's him."

"I could have killed that prick a half dozen different times when the kids were little. It never failed, one of his damn trucks always showed up just before dinner. Damn kids screaming for ten bucks worth of ice cream. Ten bucks...hell, we didn't have a dollar to our name back then. And that song still makes my blood boil, that dog song, you know? They got that chime thing going with the damn bells. Son of a bitch always seemed to park right in front of our house. God, I don't miss those days," he said, shaking his head.

"Yeah, I know what you mean."

I made a mental note not to mention Mr. Swirlee again.

"You know who works for him, or anyway he did awhile back? Bernie!" Jimmy said.

"Bernie? You mean the burnout?"

"Yeah, you got him, Bernie Sneen. You know him, right?"

"Not really, except that he's sort of missing a few cards from his deck."

Well, yeah…anyway, he was driving one of those trucks last I heard. Might explain the drug use, listening to that damn dog song chiming away, it'd drive anyone nuts."

"Bernie? They let that guy near kids?"

"Yeah, I guess so."

"God."

Chapter Three

I found Bernie Sneen in a different bar. There were at least four places he was a daily regular. He was in the third place I checked, Dizzies.

You could say Dizzies was a bit low on ambience, but then that would suggest there might be some. Dizzies was all business, and the business was drinking. The bar itself was no more than twelve feet wide from the back of the bar to the opposite wall. If you were looking for food, casual conversation, a fun night out, or pleasant company, this was not the place.

It was dim, unfriendly, and smelled like the men's room at a bus station. Bernie Sneen sat three stools in from the front door, bathed in the light of the overhead television displaying a soundless episode of "Skating with the Stars." He seemed to be muttering to himself as I climbed on the worn vinyl stool next to him.

"Hey, Bernie, long time no see. How's it going?"

He looked over at me and nodded, his lips moved, but they were apparently involved in some inner conversation. He put a hand up, signaling me to wait a moment.

"What can I get you?" the bartender asked a moment later.

"I'll have a Leinenkugel's. Give Bernie whatever he's drinking."

"Ouzo and Heineken's," the bartender replied by way of explanation.

Bernie's lips continued to move until the drinks were delivered. He raised his glass of ouzo, nodded and took a sip.

"You're that goofy P.I., right?" he asked after setting his shot glass down.

"Dev Haskell, we've talked a couple of times, I think in The Spot," I said, trying to steer things in a little more positive direction.

Bernie nodded then just stared at his beer.

Eventually I asked, "Hey, weren't you driving an ice cream truck for Mr. Swirlee?"

"That bastard," he said, shaking his head.

"Yeah, Mr. Swirlee. You still driving for him?"

"Nah, bastard laid me off. Didn't like me drinking while I was driving, I guess. Jesus, what was I supposed to do, crawling along them streets about two miles an hour."

He was quiet for a minute or two, then looked over at me and grinned idiotically. For the first time I noticed his glazed eyes blinked furtively in time to a slight facial twitch.

I nodded, suggesting he actually made some sense.

Bernie was one of those guys that no matter how you tried to clean him up he always looked like he needed a bath. At about six foot one he was two inches taller than me. I put his weight at forty pounds less, no more than one-fifty. He had dark, thinning hair, too long and slicked back against his skull. Not so much a particular style as it was just unkempt. Sallow skinned, he was in need of a shave and sported an Adam's apple

13

the size of a golf ball on his scrawny neck. Not what you'd call attractive.

"They catch you eating all the ice cream?" I joked.

"Yeah, right," he said again with the idiotic grin. I noticed a dark hole on the left side of his mouth, about four teeth back.

"You ever deal with Mr. Swirlee, himself?"

He glanced at me. I was quickly becoming an irritant now that he had finished the Ouzo and was more than halfway through the beer I'd purchased.

"That bastard? I had to talk with him when I got my route, then the night post."

"Night post?"

Bernie looked over at me, twitched a few times then stared straight ahead and sipped his Heinekens. I was definitely an annoyance.

"What do you mean, night post?"

"Look, I don't want to talk about it, if you don't mind."

"Just asking."

"You work for the cops?" he asked, then proceeded to drain his glass.

"The cops? Me? No. Just curious about the night post thing."

"And I said I didn't want to talk about it. Jesus, what is it with you?"

"Look, Bernie, I…"

"Nice chatting," he said, and jumped off his stool, twitched at me briefly, then quickly walked out into the sunshine, hands thrust deep in his pockets. I noticed his shoes. Unlaced black high tops faded almost grey, with bright red laces. Bernie was ever the trendsetter.

14

"Get you anything else?" the bartender asked. He cleared away Bernie's empty shot glasses then looked at my untouched beer.

"No thanks," I said, shaking my head. I took a cue from Bernie, climbed off the stool, and went out the door. I figured my beer wouldn't go to waste. The bartender would probably serve it to the next person who came in.

Chapter Four

I called Connie Ortiz at home a little after 7:00 that night. We'd dated a few years back until Connie came to her senses and dumped me, although it was really one of those mutually agreed decisions. We got along well, and joked when we ran into each other, which wasn't too often.

"Hi, Connie, Dev Haskell."

"Hi."

"Hey, you got a minute to chat?"

"Yeah, but really not much more than that. Kind of crazy, you know? But go ahead. What can I do for you?"

"I wanted to ask you about a business. In fact, I tried to reach you at your office earlier."

"Today? I didn't get a message."

"Well, I spoke to Sandy. She…"

"Sandy? Oh, yeah, well…I think she's still upset about that reckless driving charge a few years back."

"Yeah, I know. I got the thing pled down for her. Jesus, they were going to charge her with a DWI and leaving the scene. Under the circumstances she could have been looking at some jail time not to mention losing her license. She just can't seem to get it through her head that…"

"Well, I don't want to get into it, but you know she maintains she wasn't even behind the wheel."

"Yeah, I know. You're right we probably shouldn't get into it."

I'd always wondered since Sandy had passed out, how could she possibly remember I'd been behind the wheel?

"So, how can I help you? I'm guessing you didn't call about Sandy's driving record."

"Oh, yeah, I'm working on a project for a client. What can you tell me about Mr. Swirlee?"

"Mr. Swirlee, the ice cream business?"

"Yeah."

"Who's your client?"

"I'm going to have to interject client privilege here and not say."

"Okay, I guess. Mr. Swirlee, well, they're pretty big. I'd guess they employ over a hundred people in this town."

"What about competition?"

"Competition?"

"Yeah, is Mr. Swirlee the only show in town? I've sort of been out of the ice cream demographic for about thirty years."

"I can think of a couple of competitors, but they're really small. Competitors in name only, and I can only think of one now that I mention it. I don't know, but I would guess Mr. Swirlee has about 99-plus percent of the market."

"You ever dealt with him?"

"I've met him a couple of times over the years. Wendell something."

"Weldon," I corrected.

"Yeah, that sounds right. Like I said, I've met him, but not what you might call dealt with him. I would say he is a very focused individual."

"That's a nice way to put it."

"That's why I'm in the position I'm in."

"You know of any group or individual who might wish him harm?"

"Off the record?"

"As always."

"No, to answer your question directly. Any competition he has, on the ice cream level, would be small players. I can't see anyone doing something illegal if that's what you mean. On the other hand, as I said, he is a very focused individual. I hear he can be rather difficult…ruthless may be a better term. Of course, there have always been the rumors of the gambling thing."

"Yeah, I've heard some of those rumors, too. What do you hear on that front?" I asked, wondering gambling?

"Well, it's always been alleged he's involved in gambling, but the flip side is the term 'alleged'. To my knowledge nothing has ever been even remotely proven. I think there may have been a handful of incidents with some of his drivers, but then again, what sort of person wants to drive an ice cream truck for a career?"

I conjured up a brief image of twitching Bernie Sneen and shuddered.

"I would expect he has to be fairly careful during the hiring process. Background checks, credit checks, that sort of thing," Connie continued.

Another image of Bernie popped into my mind.

"Okay, but Connie, to your knowledge no one offers a competitive threat to him."

18

"A competitive threat to Mr. Swirlee, for ice cream? No, I can't imagine anyone providing much of a threat. It would be so expensive just to get started, let alone the overhead required with today's fuel prices. I mean he loses six months a year just with bad weather. I just can't see it. In fact, it's nothing short of amazing that he's done as well as he has. You know, who you should talk to is the Scoop people."

"Scoop people?"

"Over on the West Side, Double or Giant Scoop, something like that. I think they have a couple of trucks. They might be able to answer some of your questions. But now that I think about it, Mr. Swirlee has a fleet, and the only competitor I can think of in town has two trucks. Anyway, give them a call. Staschio Lydell or Lydella, something like that. Hey look, Dev, I've gotta run. Great chatting. Give me a call if I can be of any more help."

"Yeah, I'll call Sandy."

"Well, that might not be the best idea, but then again you can't really blame her."

"Thanks, Connie."

Chapter Five

The Giant Scoop ice cream company was located halfway down the Ohio Street hill, just across the High Bridge on the West side of St. Paul. The corporate headquarters, such as they were, were located in what looked to have been a neighborhood filling station sometime in the past. It must have been a distant past, the building was built in the late 1920s.

It was brick, painted white with faded blue trim. The roof was covered with red glazed tiles. There were two large overhead doors on the right side, one of which stood open. You could almost see a gas-station attendant waiting to fill your car, wash the windows, and check your air pressure.

Two yellow ice cream trucks emblazoned with giant ice cream cones on three sides and a triple-scoop-cone hood ornament were parked out front. Two dark-haired young women, in cutoffs and T-shirts, were loading the trucks with boxes of ice cream treats.

"Hi, I'm looking for Staschio," I said, following up with my charming smile.

"He's not here," one of the girls said. Neither one stopped stacking the cardboard boxes into the rear of the trucks. They must have missed my smile. They looked alike, and I guessed they might be sisters.

"Do you expect him anytime soon?"

"Not really," the one closest to me said.

She stopped what she was doing, wiped her hands on the dark green apron around her waist and stuck out her hand to shake.

"Sorry, I'm Jill. She's my sister, Annie." She nodded at the girl still loading boxes into the back of the other truck.

"Dev Haskell," I said, shaking her hand. She had a firm grip, dark brown eyes and a bright smile.

"Hey," Annie said, nodding in my direction, but not stopping her work.

"Our grandfather isn't here, and we're kinda busy getting ready for the day. What's this about?"

I took out a couple of my business cards, and handed them to Jill.

"Haskell Investigations, Devlin Haskell, private investigator," she read then looked up at me.

Annie stopped loading ice cream and took one of the cards from Jill.

"Is there some kind of trouble?"

"No, nothing like that. I'm just trying to learn more about the business and thought your grandfather might be able to help."

"Learn more about the ice cream truck business? Why?" Annie asked.

"Yeah, what on earth for? Thinking of making a career change or something?" Jill laughed.

"No, just curious about what you do."

"Look, we sell twelve different ice cream treats, usually to kids," Jill said, pointing at a menu painted on the back of the truck.

"We pay too much for product, pay too much for gas and taxes. Get raped by the city for a license. And by the time we repair whatever the latest breakdown will be on these trucks we have just about enough left over to pay ourselves almost a dollar an hour."

I looked from Jill to Annie.

"That's about right," Annie said. "Except I think you're a little high on the hourly wage part."

"Tell you what…you got the time you can ride along with me today. That'll answer just about any questions you might have," Jill said.

"Ride along with you? You mean in the truck?" I asked.

"No, on top of it. Yes in the truck. You up for it?"

"Well, I don't know. I got a couple of other appointments that…"

Jill glanced over at the Lincoln Town Car I'd parked on the street, dark green, except for the light blue door on the passenger side. Then there was the slightly buckled hood where a brick wall had jumped in front of me one night.

"Yeah sure, appointments. You don't have shit to do, do you?"

"I might."

"Come on, I could use the company."

Annie was shaking her head as she wheeled the empty cart back into one of the garage bays. She pushed a button to automatically lower the overhead door and walked back to her truck.

"I'll catch you two later," she said.

"So?" Jill asked me.

"Yeah, I guess…sure, why not?"

Chapter Six

Jill didn't have a chime playing some obnoxious child's song on her truck. Instead, there was a bell that rang every thirty seconds. I wasn't sure which was worse.

"This bell-ringing all day would drive me nuts," I said, raising my voice to be heard over the damned bell.

Jill smiled and shook her head.

"Believe it or not, you get used to it. Tell you the truth, I don't even hear it anymore. Although, it is nice to get home at the end of the day to peace and quiet with maybe just the clock ticking."

She was driving slowly along a residential street. Kids waved, and you could see them running into the house, theoretically to ask for money. Occasionally moms and kids flagged us down. Sometimes kids on bikes followed us. Despite Jimmy the bartender's reaction, everyone I watched seemed genuinely glad to see us.

"Where do you live?" I asked.

"Just across the alley from the shop. It was my folks' house. We grew up there. You?"

"St. Paul, close to the Cathedral."

Jill nodded, then pulled to the curb as three kids waved currency and jumped up and down excitedly. Over the course of a few hours I handled the sales. Cherry and Root Beer Ice Bergs seemed to be big sellers. But then, of course, there was the always popular Fudgesicle. Eventually I got around to my client.

"So how do you guys stack up against Mr. Swirlee?"

"That prick?"

"You're not a fan?"

"Let's just say no, and leave it at that."

"So he's the big success everyone is gunning for?" I asked.

Jill looked over her shoulder at me. I was sitting sideways on a card table chair, leaning against a cooler filled with all the ice cream treats.

"Not really. I'm sure that jerk doesn't even know we exist. I mean we've been out here for what?" She checked her watch. "Over four and a half hours. You've seen the amount of business we've done and for a weekday this has been pretty good. I oughta bring you along more often. You're good luck." She smiled.

"Have you ever met the guy?"

"You mean, Mr. Swirlee himself? No. He and my grandfather started out as partners, about a thousand years ago. Grandpa never talks about it, but he got screwed somehow. We just do our deal over here, in this neighborhood. Mr. Swirlee covers the rest of the world." She half laughed and pulled over for a fat kid at the curb.

It came as no surprise the kid knew the menu by heart.

"Give me a Banana Ice Burg, a Chocolate Ice Cream Sandwich and a Giant Dilly bar, please."

It took me a moment to total things up. The Dilly Bar threw me. It was the first one I'd sold, two twenty-five each. The kid waited, drumming his fat little fingers on the counter impatiently, while I attempted to total things up in my head.

"That'll be six dollars and seventy-five cents," I said cheerily.

The kid glanced down at the exact change he'd laid on the counter almost five minutes earlier, six dollars and fifty cents. He shot a fake smile in my direction, snatched up the ice cream treats, and fled the scene.

"Just what that kid needs, more ice cream. Want me to go after him?" I asked watching him waddle around the corner of a house.

"No, he's a good customer. Besides, he was right it was six-fifty not six-seventy-five," Jill said as she pulled away from the curb.

"So, you were telling me your grandfather was in business with Mr. Swirlee."

"That's the story. I guess there was some sort of a falling out. I don't really know anything about it. We just do our own thing. Is that who you're working for? Mr. Swirlee?"

"Me, Mr. Swirlee? What makes you think that?"

"I don't know. Maybe because it's about the fourth time you've mentioned him. Maybe because I can't think of who else would be interested in our business and now that you've seen it you can report back to your boss that there isn't that much of it."

"He's not my boss," I shot back.

"So you are working for the creep. I should have known. What? I suppose he's gonna move a couple of trucks into our area. Jesus, you jerk. I'll take you back. I'm sure you have a report to give him just as soon as possible." I rocked back against the cooler as she accelerated down the street.

"Hey, calm down, Jill. No, it's nothing like that at all. If you want the truth, I'll tell you, no need to get all offended," I said, stalling for time, doing a quick reassessment.

"Sure you will," she said, and sped up even more, clearly not convinced.

"I just met the guy the other day. He hired me to find out who attempted to kill him."

"What? Someone tried to kill that piece of poop? Fantastic!"

"Sorry to be the one to break the news. I can tell you're distressed," I said.

"You just made my day. Wait till I tell Annie, she'll freak."

"Yeah, well, the bad news is, I don't think that's what happened."

"What do you mean?"

"Mr. Swirlee got pretty banged up in a car accident, broke a leg or something. He'll recover, but…"

"Damn!"

"He'll recover, but I think it was just a hit and run he just happened to get hit. I can't believe anyone was out to get him."

"Why not? The guy is an absolute butt hole, ask anyone," she said.

"Hey, that seems to be the common perception, I get that part. But his being dead, would that improve your business any? If he had been killed, would you or your sister sell anymore ice cream today as opposed to last week at this time?"

"Well, no."

"So, even though the guy is a jerk, which seems to be the universal conclusion, I don't see anyone in the ice cream business crossing over the sane lane trying to kill the guy."

She glanced back at me for a long moment, then returned to her driving, shaking her head.

"You better get your facts straight. I wasn't thinking about his ice cream business."

"What do you mean?"

"You said you work for the guy?" she asked.

"Yeah, sort of, I already told you that."

"You better check with the cops. I know, I know, they can't prove anything, but we have a pretty good idea of what the profit margins are in this business. Lose a dollar a day and make it up on volume, it just doesn't add up."

"What are you saying?" I asked.

"What I'm saying is, here we are. You can get out here. Thanks for riding along. Sorry it didn't work out better, but you should have been up front with me," she said, then pulled alongside my Lincoln, stopped, and stared straight ahead.

"Look, Jill, I'm sorry. I didn't mean to upset you," I said.

"It's okay, I'm not upset, honest. But I've got to get back to work so you better hop out."

"Okay, it's been interesting. Thanks for your time and the help," I said exiting. I was halfway out of the rear door when she accelerated and sent me stumbling into the street. By the time I was on my feet she'd rounded the corner, and the sound of the clanging bell grew fainter.

Chapter Seven

"No, Sir, like I said before, they're gone. He checked out sometime last night. I came in this morning and learned they'd left."

I was talking with the station nurse on the wing where Mr. Swirlee had been. She didn't seem at all upset that he was off her floor.

"He couldn't have healed up that quickly, could he? I mean, I thought he had a broken leg. You guys had him immobilized with some cushion things, and he was on medications or painkillers or something."

"I know. Actually a broken ankle, by the way. We recommended he not leave, but if the patient insists on wanting to check out, well, at some point there's nothing we can do about it. Can't say we tried too hard to change his mind," she added, the disdain in her tone apparent.

"Difficult patient?"

"Difficult couple. Look, I've got twenty-seven patients I'm responsible for on this wing. All of them have needs, questions, medications and scheduled procedures. I can't station myself at any one door and wait to be at someone's beck and call. That would be rather unfair now, wouldn't it?"

"Yes, I suppose so."

"So the Swirlmanns decided they would receive better care if they hired someone in their home. They're probably right, provided there aren't any complications and they employ qualified individuals. You have to have people who know and understand what should be done. There are inherent risks on all sides of the equation," she said, then gave me a perfunctory nod.

"I see."

"Will there be anything else, Mr. Haskell?"

"No, you've been quite helpful. Thank you."

Chapter Eight

I phoned Mr. Swirlee. Lola's little girl's voice answered after I'd lost count of the rings.

"Hi, Mrs. Swirlmann, this is Dev Haskell."

There was a long pause.

"The private eye. We met yesterday in your husband's hospital room," I added.

"Oh, you," she half squealed.

"Yeah, I was able to clear some time on my calendar," I lied. "I was wondering if I could stop over and speak with your husband. Go over some facts, see if I could learn anything else from either of you."

"Well, he'd be the one to talk to about that," she said.

"Coming over?"

"No, learning something. What time did you have in mind?"

"The sooner, the better. I've got some time later today, if that would work," I looked at my empty beer glass and nodded at Jimmy for another.

"We'll be waiting."

"Wait, you haven't…well I'm not exactly sure where you …" I blurted just before she hung up.

I phoned her back, got the address on one of the city's most prominent streets, Summit Avenue, then sipped my late lunch and wondered what in the hell I was going to ask Mr. Swirlee.

Chapter Nine

The house on Summit Avenue was a brick three-story structure built about 1890. It had a slate roof, dormers on all sides and looked imperious. A seven-foot wrought-iron fence, updated with security cameras, surrounded the manicured yard. Two large black Dobermans lay in the sun on the front steps. Just in case you didn't get the message, a sign on the front gate stated in large red letters "No trespassing or solicitors."

There was a phone mounted on one of the brick pillars at the front gate. The moment I picked the receiver up I heard the audible whir of a camera overhead. As it turned and sighted in on me, a small green light on the camera began to blink. I listened to the phone ringing somewhere on the other end for what seemed to be ten minutes. Eventually it was picked up.

I could hear breathing but no words.

"This is Devlin Haskell, to see Mr. and Mrs. Swirlmann," I said.

"I'll let you in," a squeaky female voice replied. There was a buzz and the gate lock made an audible click. I hung up the phone, pushed open the gate, stepped in, then pulled the gate closed behind me.

The heads on both Dobermans snapped to attention for just half a second before they flew off the front steps, racing toward me, barking and growling. They were large, sleek and looked identical as they flew toward me, black with brown muzzles, black leather collars with silver spikes and very large white fangs. I tugged on the gate, but the electronic lock had reengaged and I was caught inside. They covered the fifty feet from the front steps to me in just a second or two. I turned to face them as they came alongside with throaty growls, one drooling a trail of droplets on the sidewalk. Rabies?

"Oh, God," I whimpered and hoped they'd been recently fed. I reminded myself they were capable of smelling fear and began to slowly walk as unthreateningly as possible toward the front door. Eventually, I made it to the front steps and reached up to ring the doorbell, which set off more vicious barking and snarling. If I was supposed to feel intimidated, it worked. I waited for what seemed like a lifetime before the front door finally opened.

"Oh, Mr. Haskell," Lola squeaked over the growling monsters. She sounded genuinely surprised to see me, although I'd spoken to her just a minute before. The dogs held their ground, but increased the tempo and viciousness of their barking. Lola continued to stand in the doorway and smile, either oblivious of, or thoroughly enjoying my predicament.

"Could I please come in?" I pleaded in a squeaky voice that rivaled hers.

She stepped aside then eventually closed the door behind me.

"Nice dogs," I said, trying to swallow my heart back down while they barked and snarled on the far side of the door. I peeked out the lace curtained window and one of them lunged at me.

"Aren't they sweet? Follow me, we're in the study," she said, turning to walk down an immense oak-paneled hall. I followed, still shaking as the occasional throaty bark rumbled on the far side of the front door.

Lola had some sort of sparkle makeup dusted on her shoulders and chest. She wore white stretch pants that looked tight enough to be a second skin. A bouncing halter top sort of affair about four sizes too small was stretched as tight as possible and wonderfully failed to cover.

Her feet, with painted toenails and gold toe rings were strapped to jeweled, spike-heeled sandals. The heels forced her to take very tiny steps. The slightest hint of a tiny red thong occasionally showed through the stretch pants as she wiggled down the long hall.

She turned and went through a large entry with a sliding door. The elaborate woodwork surrounding the massive doorway was carved with a series of ice cream cones.

"Precious, that man is here," she said to Mr. Swirlee who was propped up in a hospital bed in front of the window. He had what appeared to be a walking cast on his left leg and a phone against his right ear. He gave a perfunctory nod in my direction then continued shouting into his phone.

"No, didn't you hear me the first time? I told you we'll have to push it back by at least a week. I can't get a straight answer out of any of these quacks. They're telling me months. I don't have that kind of time. So move it back a week, to next Wednesday."

As he shouted, I glanced around the study. All four walls had elegant, dark wooden bookcases standing to a height of about seven feet. The remaining seven feet, up to the elaborate plaster ceiling was covered with oil paintings in heavy gilt frames, all horses. I guessed each painting was probably worth more than my reported take in any given year. Eventually, Mr. Swirlee screamed into the phone then hung up and glared at me.

"So, tell me what you found out. Well?" he snarled, then dialed his phone and slapped it against his ear.

I could have told him the few people I had spoken with referred to him as a bastard, a prick, a butt hole, someone ruthless and difficult. Not exactly a ringing personality endorsement, not that Mr. Swirlee would have cared.

"Well, Sir, it's not quite so simple. Bit more of a complex issue ..."

"Gary, hang on, I'm dealing with some bullshit here." He spit into his phone, then glared at me again.

"You got a name for me?"

"A name?"

"Jesus, save me!" He sighed. "Do you know who did this? Any idea who tried to kill me?"

"I'm not sure anyone did try. Like I said yesterday, it could have been a simple hit-and-run. I've barely gotten start ..."

"Barely gotten started! Is that what you were going to say? What the hell do you think I'm paying you to do? Stand around looking stupid? You got that part down. Get your ass out of here and find out who in the hell was behind this."

"I'll see you out." Lola said and was on her feet, taking tiny steps toward the door.

"Yeah, Gary!" Swirlee was back on the phone as we exited the room. "No, just some idiot who can't get the job done. I know, I know…"

We were almost to the front door. I was thinking of the dogs when I wasn't thinking of Lola walking ahead of me.

"You have to excuse him, he's usually such a little pussycat," she said, turning toward me and giving me a little shoulder shrug that caused a lot of bouncing and ended in a big smile.

I was having a tough time with all of it.

"Look, Mrs. Swirlmann…"

"Oh, please, call me Lola. I'd like that," she half whispered, just the hint of a raised eyebrow.

"Okay, look, Lola, to tell you the truth, I'll check things out, but I want to be up front. I'm just not sure there's anything here. The fact that your husband didn't file a police report doesn't help matters. The people I have talked to really can't see anyone trying to hurt him to improve their ice cream business. It just doesn't seem to add up."

"The ice cream business?" she asked.

"Yeah, right. Why? Is there something else I should know about?"

"Well, we have a lot of investments, property, all sorts of things."

I got the feeling she was being purposely vague.

"Look, could I set up an appointment with your husband? If I could come back and talk to him without interruptions I might be able to make some progress. No hospital monitors, no phone calls, just the two of us, and you, if you think it would help. Maybe I could get an idea of something to go on, but right now, I've got nothing. And, well, there's the matter of a contract.

So far I've been doing some general legwork, but I would like to enter into a contract agreement."

"I see," she said in a way that made me think she really didn't.

"Can I set up an appointment through you, or a secretary, or someone who…"

"I think I can do that."

I wasn't so sure.

"All right, when would be a good time to sit down with him?"

"Why don't you plan on joining us for dinner tonight, if that would work for you?"

I had nothing going other than Jameson Night down at The Spot.

"You just tell me what time, and I'll cancel my meeting and make sure I'm here."

"Say eight o'clock?"

"I'll be here."

She placed her hand on the doorknob.

"Say, about the dogs, would there be another way out?"

"Another way?" She sounded surprised.

"Yeah, the dogs…I hate to bother them, get them all worked up, you know?"

"Oh, they're just doing their job."

"And let me tell you, they do it very well. But if there was another way out, you know, so I don't upset them too much. Besides, a little longer walk around the block would do me good…the exercise, you know?"

She considered that a moment, then said, "Come on, I'll let you out the patio door. But you'll have to be quiet. If they hear you, they can run around to the back."

I followed her down the hallway, enveloped in a cloud of her perfume, past the study door where I heard Mr. Swirlee screaming on the phone at his current victim.

We passed a massive carved staircase with two naked brass figures balancing on the newel posts then wandered into a formal dining room with a fireplace that could fit a king-size bed. We exited through a swinging door on the far side, and crossed a large kitchen with black granite countertops and white lace curtains to the rear patio doors.

From this vantage point, the manicured back lawn looked peaceful. There was a large flagstone patio, lawn chairs, a fountain, terraced gardens and beautiful flower beds. It looked like a world away from the two meat-eating monsters no doubt still drooling for me by the front door.

"How's this?" she squeaked and then gave another little shoulder shrug.

"Nice."

"No one even knows we're back here. We're all alone."

She stood very still and stared at me with just the hint of a smile on her face. I could hear her panting. Or was that me?

The little voice in my head said, *'Don't even think of trying something.'* For once, I listened.

"Where's the back gate?" I asked, studying the far garden wall.

"Over there, in the corner. See, next to the roses, the climbers," she said and leaned into me, placing her thumb firmly down the small of my back.

"The…the…the pink ones?"

"Yeah, no one can see you coming or going. It's really private, almost secret. I can take all my clothes off and just lay in the sun," she said and stared at me again, wide eyed. Her breathing seemed to be getting heavier. "Course then I need help getting the lotion in all the right spots." She smiled and just stared.

"Okay, I'll be back tonight at eight for dinner. We can all talk then. No interruptions, right?" I said, just wanting to get out of there before I did something stupid.

She sighed, nodded, then opened the patio door and leaned very close to me.

I could feel her breath on my face and stared down at all the lucky little sparkles collected in her cleavage.

"Remember, be very quiet so the dogs don't hear you," she said.

"Not to worry," I replied and left quickly.

I was a bit more than midway across the lawn, maybe thirty yards from the back gate when she called out.

"See you tonight, Mr. Haskell. See you tonight. Bye, bye." She half laughed.

The first two barks were distant, the third not quite so, and I had the frightening sense they were already on the run. So was I. Fear was a big motivator, and I had already made it to the gate just as they cleared the rear corner of the house. They looked left and right wildly, not sure where their prey was hiding.

I wasn't hiding. I was pulling furiously on the locked gate. Even from that distance they must have smelled my panic because they stretched out and raced across the lawn, teeth bared. They zeroed in on me like laser-guided missiles, howling.

In one frightened leap I was almost over the seven-foot iron fence, balancing clumsily on the top as I turned to drop to safety on the other side. Just as I went off the top, they leapt. I dropped to the ground on the far side as they slammed against the wrought iron then bounced off and landed on their backs in the middle of one of the massive climbing roses. They yelped loudly as they scrambled bloody and torn through the vicious, razor sharp rose thorns.

"Serves you right. Not so funny now, is it, ya bastards?" I said, talking tough from the safe side of the fence. I glanced toward the house and caught the hint of movement just as Lola dropped a lace window curtain.

Chapter Ten

I dressed casually for the evening, a reasonably clean sport coat and an ironed polo shirt touting the Emporium of Dance in a crest over my left breast. I didn't know if I should bring a bottle of wine as a hostess gift or a Taser to deal with the dogs. I compromised with a thirty-eight snub in the small of my back and a copy of a contract. I arrived at 8:15, stylishly late because the Lincoln was running on fumes, and I really didn't think I could make it to Mr. Swirlee's unless I filled up.

I phoned from the front gate, then waited another interminable length of time listening to the ringing on the other end. Eventually, Lola answered sounding very surprised someone was even calling.

"Hello?"

"Hi, Lola, Dev Haskell. Sorry I'm late."

"Yes?"

"Yes, Devlin Haskell. Remember, we had a dinner meeting at eight tonight with Mr. Swirlee and myself…well, and you, if you were planning to join us."

"Tonight?"

"Yeah, we arranged it this afternoon, in your front hall, before you let me out the patio door." I didn't add before you set your dogs after me. I waited.
Eventually, the gate unlocked, but I didn't move.

"What about your dogs? Are they out here? Have they been fed?" I asked.

I heard another buzz and then an audible click as the gate unlocked again, no response from the phone.

I entered the front yard. Still holding the gate open. I called, "Here boy, here boy, come on, come on. Here doggies, come here."

Nothing moved. Were they waiting to trap me in the open between the house and the gate? I wouldn't be surprised.

"Here boy, here boy, where are you?"

I whistled a couple of times.

"What in the hell do you think you're doing?" Mr. Swirlee yelled from the front door. He was standing, both hands on a chrome walker and watching me with beady eyes.

"I was just wondering about your dogs. I didn't see them and…"

"They're not here. Someone attacked them this afternoon. We had to call the paramedics, rush them to the vet."

"The paramedics?"

"Yes, the paramedics! You have any idea what in the hell those damn things cost me? They… look, just get the hell in here. The next thing you know I'll be catching a cold with this damned door open while you drag your ass whistling for the dogs that aren't here. Jesus!"

It was eighty-two degrees at the moment.

I cautiously walked to the front door and Mr. Swirlee. I was not at all sure it wasn't a setup and the two dogs were waiting just inside to attack me at any moment.

"Come on, get the hell in here. I've been waiting for dinner. You're late and I'm famished. Close the damned door behind you," he called over his shoulder as I climbed the front steps. He was already pushing his walker down the massive hall to the rear of the house.

I wondered what it would be like eating in their formal dining room. Would we dine on fine crystal, the best wine, silver serving pieces and utensils, exquisite china, a linen tablecloth and linen napkins? Did they have a butler? A chef?

"Since it's just you, we're eating in the kitchen. Lola's cooking," Mr. Swirlee scoffed as a warning that answered my questions. We groped our way across the darkened dining room and through the swinging door.

AC/DC screaming "Night Prowler" blared into the kitchen from speakers hidden somewhere.

"I told you to turn that shit off, damn it," Mr. Swirlee shouted over the noise. Lola was seated at the kitchen counter.

She was sipping from a can of Busch light and looked not to be on her first. Her bleached hair was pulled back, but long wisps had come loose and hung down. She had lost the skin glitter from earlier in the day and wore a different top, though no less form fitting. She stuck out her tongue and made a face behind Mr. Swirlee as he wheeled past, then picked up a remote and brought blessed silence to the room with a simple click.

"Jesus Christ," Mr. Swirlee exclaimed, but said nothing else.

Lola returned to her sipping.

"Get me a beer out of the fridge there. I suppose you can grab one for yourself," he said grudgingly, then groaned onto a kitchen stool and pushed his walker off to the side.

"I can't wait to be rid of this damn thing. So, please tell me you found something out, you're hot on the trail, something, anything," he said as he tore the lid off the tub of Kentucky Fried Chicken resting on the kitchen counter.

I was leaning into the massive refrigerator, virtually empty except for two cans of Busch light, a box of baking soda, and a tray of what looked like suppositories. I grabbed the beers and closed the refrigerator.

"Well, I've done some preliminary checking and I haven't found anyone of real interest, but I have managed to eliminate a number of individuals." I was thinking Jill and Annie couldn't be bothered, the nurses from the hospital were too busy, and Connie Ortiz wasn't interested.

"Eliminate? That doesn't help," he said, spitting a mouthful of chicken leg and secret batter in my direction.

"Who do you think it could be?" I asked. I took a couple of healthy sips from the beer can and understood why the stuff was so inexpensive.

"Who do I...Jesus, I don't have any idea. I just know that car didn't come out of nowhere. All of a sudden it headed straight on and rammed us. If that ain't attempted murder, I don't know what is."

I decided this was the time to get things nailed down, so I reached inside my sport coat, pulled out my contract, and tossed it on the kitchen counter in front of him.

"What the hell is this? I thought you said you didn't have a list," he snarled. Then he reached into the red-and-white tub for another drumstick and shoved the entire thing into his mouth.

"It's not a list. That's my contract. You want me to do any investigating for you, I'll need you to sign my contract. Up till now you haven't told me a thing, other than you think someone tried to kill you. No offense, but virtually everyone in town is a suspect. It's been two days, and I'm not running across a lot of people who are fans."

"Jealous is what the bastards are," he said spitting more chicken and batter across the counter.

Lola got off her stool and lurched toward a side doorway and down a hall. She had changed from the sprayed-on stretch pants to a pair of sprayed-on shorts.

I stopped staring and said, "Maybe they're jealous. But, I'm sure you, of all people, understand I really can't do any more for you until I have a signed contract. It protects both of us," I added.

He thought about that for a moment.

"So I sign this, and you find out who tried to kill me. That it?"

"No, you sign, and I investigate." I reached into my pocket, took out a business card and handed it to him.

"Haskell Investigations?" he said looking up at me surprised, like it was the first time he'd heard the name.

"Yeah, it's what I do. I investigate. I try and present you with facts, not rumors, not guesses, but facts, from which you might be able to make a more informed decision."

"Yeah, well, Lola actually takes care of this sort of thing for me."

"Lola?" I said, unable to keep the surprise out of my voice.

"What?" she said from the doorway behind me. She walked unsteadily back to her stool, carrying an unopened can of beer, sat down heavily, then pulled the tab off the can. Beer sprayed over the contract and across the counter, though neither of them acknowledged the fact.

"Here, read this, see what you think," Mr. Swirlee said, pushing my contract through the beer puddle toward Lola.

"So, what you're telling me is you may not be able to tell me a damn thing. But I'll still have to pay you. Is that it?" Swirlee asked.

Lola was off her stool, opened a drawer behind her, pulled out a pair of eyeglasses and a pen and then returned to her stool, her beer, and my contract.

"Well, not exactly."

"Humph, nice work if you can get it," he scoffed.

"I'll do my best to explore all options. You suggest someone tried to kill you. Okay, I'll examine that possibility. But, I also want to look at the possibility of a simple hit-and-run. Maybe it was someone who was drinking, or someone who panicked, or some guy who was just a lousy driver. Just maybe it was some guy who has no idea who you are, you know?"

"You weren't there, and I know," he grumbled.

"There," Lola said, weaving on her stool as she finished signing my contract with a lavender-colored marker in a signature about four inches high. She pushed the contract back to me through the puddle of beer, causing the purple signature to run.

"Did you even read the damn thing?" Mr. Swirlee scoffed.

"Yes," she said, eyes flashing as she pushed the soggy document farther across the counter toward me.

Mr. Swirlee shook his head.

"Come on, I'll show you out," he said as he slid off his stool and grasped his walker.

"Let me ask you a couple of questions first. I'd like to get a handle on exactly what happened the other night. You said you thought someone was following you?"

"Not tonight, I've got another meeting. Lets go, I'll show you out," he said, pushing his walker out the kitchen door and into the darkened dining room. He was still holding a chicken drumstick in his left hand.

"Always nice to chat with you, Lola. Thanks for the beer," I said.

"Bye-bye," she said, and then waved.

At the front door Mr. Swirlee, ever the gracious gentleman, said, "Okay, you got your damned contract signed. Now find out who in the hell tried to kill me the other night. And I don't want any more bullshit excuses." Then he opened the front door and before I knew what had happened I was outside on the steps. He slammed the door behind me and turned off the porch light.

__Chapter Eleven__

I made it down to The Spot for Jameson Night a little before ten. Two-for-one shots. I hadn't been there for more than a couple of minutes when I saw a familiar, unattractive face and grabbed an empty stool next to him.

"Well, Bernie Sneen, twice in two days. I wonder who I pissed off to deserve this."

Bernie looked up at me, glassy eyed, taking a long while to focus. He wore a St. Paul Saints baseball cap slightly off center, just like Bernie.

"Oh, you, Dribble, right? You ever find out who tried to take out that prick Swirlee?"

"It's Devlin," I corrected, took out a business card and placed it on the bar in front of him.

"Haskell Investigations, shit. So, you catch the guy?"

"No, to answer your question, I'm still sorting that out. I'm not so sure it wasn't just an accident. Although to tell you the truth, it could be anyone. Nobody seems to like the guy. The more I look, the longer the suspect list. Everyone feels just like you whenever I mention Swirlee." I thought maybe I could play Bernie as a pal.

"Well, you got that part right. You know something? He's not a very nice guy. His chick's even worse," Bernie said and then made a show of searching his pockets for another three dollars to buy two more shots.

"I'll get it. Both of us," I said, tossing a ten on the bar.

"Gee, thanks…always thought you were kind of a jerk, who knew?" Bernie giggled, then waved his head in my direction and stared bleary eyed.

"You know his wife?" I asked.

"Wife? She ain't his wife. She's just his current entertainment. Just don't trust her, is all."

"Why's that?" I asked.

Bernie stared straight ahead, ignoring me.

"And you told me you used to work for Mr. Swirlee. Drove one of his trucks? Driving for him must have been tough."

Bernie seemed to shudder slightly.

"Thanks, Carey," I said to the bartender as the shots appeared in front of us.

"You don't know the half of it. All those shitty kids, the goddamn little dog chime. Jesus Christ, if the song don't drive you nuts, them parents threatening to kill you if you don't get out of there will do the trick. Then working those late nights."

"Yeah, you were gonna tell me about the night spot," I said, raising a shot glass to Bernie. "Here's to you, buddy. Glad you don't have to put up with Mr. Swirlee anymore."

"Thanks, man. Yeah, the night spot, Jesus, guys wanting to place, then arguing about the odds and shit. Bastard Swirlee said I was stealing from him. I told him I didn't, leastwise I was gonna put it back, soon as I got the cash, you know? I meant it to be a little loan, is all. Like just overnight or something. That really ain't stealing. Besides, she made me pay her. You know how it is."

I nodded like I knew, then raised the shot glass to Bernie again. He was already onto his second shot and tossed it down without so much as a blink.

"But that weren't good enough for your pal, that bastard Swirlee, no Sir."

"The bastard," I agreed, pushing my second shot toward Bernie and giving him the okay with a slight nod.

"Thanks," he said, then tossed it down, held the glass up for a long moment until the last drop eventually ran down the inside of the glass and fell into his mouth.

"I'll bet he didn't like that," I said.

"Bastard took the first one just because, said he couldn't let the word get out. I told him I sure as hell wasn't gonna tell anyone," Bernie half sobbed, then thrust his right hand along the bar toward me. The little finger, ring finger and half his middle finger were missing.

"I didn't have the cash." He was suddenly crying, getting a little louder.

"Hey, look, Bernie..."

"I mean, fifty bucks, big deal. I'm good for it, right? She told me no one would ever know. So the next day, he shows up at my joint. Has some goons kick my door in. The crazy bitch is with him and these really mean dogs, barking and growling...big bastards." Bernie visibly shuddered, then continued.

"I told him I'd pay, he takes another finger anyway. Let's her feed it to them dogs. She's standing there like she's innocent or something. Swirlee tells me I owe him interest. Hundred bucks a day, he says.

What was I gonna do? I can't hide. He'd find me. So I got the dough, two hundred and fifty bucks. Don't even ask me how. Paid the bastard and he takes half of the next finger. A reminder, he says, like I needed a reminder, Jesus God!" Bernie sobbed loudly, tears rolled down his dirty face.

A couple of guys in a booth behind us were watching, mouths open. We were clearly ruining their buzz.

"Two more for Bernie here," I called quickly, trying to get things centered back on cheap liquor and moving in a more positive direction.

"Bernie, you okay?" Carey asked.

Bernie thrust his hand back under the bar, nodded, then waited for the next round.

"Those guys at the night spot…they were placing bets, right? And Lola, she just wanted a good time." I made it a statement, rather than a question.

"What in the hell do you think I've been talking about? She said no one would know. Said she was into freaks like me. Jesus, talk about a freak, you shoulda seen her. Anyway, you think all them guys wanted ice cream for fuck's sake? That it? They were coming up at night with a couple hundred bucks and they wanted ice cream? Shit."

"Then she has me follow them coming home the other night. Told me to ram him. I was gonna, but I chickened out at the last minute."

"What?"

"Ha, ha, ha, ha…" He sort of laughed, but insanely, there was nothing funny sounding about it. He suddenly lurched off the bar stool, took two steps back, and looked at me.

"Oh where, oh where has my little dog gone? Oh where, oh where can he be?" Bernie screeched over Bob Segar on the jukebox.

"Oh, oh," Carey said and gave the nod to a rather large guy who gently took Bernie by the arm and ushered him outside.

"With his ears so short and his tail…"

"Jesus, Carey, I had no idea. I'm sorry. I didn't know he'd go off like that. All of a sudden he's…"

"Relax, Dev. It happens sometimes. He's damaged goods, you know? It's just real bad for business when he gets like that. Sort of ruins the glow around here, if you know what I mean. Get you another?"

I nodded yes.

Carey returned with two more shots.

"Yeah, it's too bad. Poor guy was in some sort of industrial accident awhile back and just never got over it. Not that he was playing with a full deck to begin with, but…"

"Industrial accident?" I asked.

"Yeah, lost some fingers. I don't know if you noticed or not. Probably a log-splitter or something like that. Not exactly the first guy who'd come to mind for following OSHA recommendations, you know?"

Bernie's tale of Mr. Swirlee, Lola, and the dogs rang truer than Carey's log-splitter version. Now I was curious.

Chapter Twelve

Once again I remained at The Spot longer than I should have, and then decided it would be a good idea at almost two in the morning to find Bernie's old night spot.

I found one of Mr. Swirlee's trucks parked on East Sixth Street, just behind the Holiday gas station. The downtown location seemed a strange place to try and sell ice cream at two thirty on a Thursday morning.

I parked in front of a white Escalade, opposite the ice cream truck. At least it wasn't playing the chime that helped drive Bernie Sneen literally off his rocker.

"What'll it be?" the attendant rasped at me as I approached the window. He had a laptop open, the blue glare off the screen lighting his large bald head so it appeared to be floating like a full moon. No doubt he was social networking on the computer.

He had a large black mustache and sported small gold earrings in both ears. The S-curve along the bridge of his nose suggested the occasional difference of opinion. He wore a black T-shirt over heavy shoulders that stretched across even heavier biceps. His hands looked like hams, with fingers made from construction rebar. A blue, blurry homemade tattoo adorned the back of each hand. I guessed he got the tattoos in a state institution, not the U of M.

"Give me a Fudgesicle." I grinned, remembering the fat kid the day I was riding around with Jill.

"What?"

"A Fudgesicle."

"Get the hell out of here," he scoffed.

"Okay, okay, just checking. I need to place a bet."

He eyed me warily, then asked,

"You got a name?"

"A name, you mean like Bernie Sneen or Mr. Swirlee? Come on, what kind of odds you got? Tell me that, then I can give you a name." I was beginning to enjoy this.

"I think you better leave, Sir."

"Aw, come on, be a pal. I'm just screwing around. Look what can I bet on tonight? I need a sure winner, you know?"

"Actually, no, I don't know. I got no idea what in the hell you're talking about," he said and slid a little window closed, then sat back down in his chair.

I knocked on the window. I'd clearly gotten to him and even in my over-served state I knew I was onto something here.

"Hey, hey, buddy, open up. Hey, come on, man, open up," I called then tugged on the window. Apparently he'd locked it.

I heard footsteps behind me, turned and faced two fairly large individuals. Certainly larger than me, they wore blue jeans, black T-shirts like the guy in the truck, and had the definite shape of bodybuilders. One had a crew cut and a dopey look, the other wore glasses and had his hair pulled back in a ponytail. He had those sideburn things, the kind that followed the jaw line and tapered down to a fine point, like knives

54

on either side of his face. They stood with their feet apart, arms loose at their sides. They were close but not on top of me. They clearly knew what they were doing.

"Jesus, the guy won't open up for me," I said by way of explanation.

"Can we help you, Sir?"

"Help me? No, not really. I just wanted to place an order is all, and Baldy in there won't open up."

One of them looked over my shoulder into the ice cream truck. My gaze followed. The thug inside the truck shook his head no.

"I guess he's closed for the night. Maybe you should just head home. Probably be a good idea."

"No, I don't think I'll do that. I want a goddamned Fudgesicle, and I'm not leaving until…"

It happened so fast I wasn't sure which one had hit me. Whoever it was, he'd knocked me to the ground, and as I rolled onto my knees a boot kicked me in the ribs, hard. Steel toes based on the bruise I received. One of them jerked me to my feet effortlessly. I smelled garlic as he held me up on my tiptoes and very close to his face.

I reached under my sport coat into the small of my back and pulled out the snub thirty-eight. Then I lifted his chin with the barrel just to get his attention. It worked. He let go and slowly took a step backward.

"Not such a tough…"

"Move another inch, and you're all over the street," a voice behind me rasped. Baldy, in the ice cream truck racked a round into the chamber. An unmistakable sound, especially when your back was to it.

I remained very still.

My two assailants backed off to the side and out of the line of fire. I followed their movement with the thirty-eight, but otherwise remained perfectly still.

"Probably be a good idea if you calmly got your dumb ass back in your car and drove away, while you still can," Baldy advised from inside the ice cream truck.

"Swirlee's gonna hear about this," I bluffed.

"Get the hell out of here," Baldy said.

I slowly walked away, keeping the thirty-eight pointed in the general direction of the two idiots on the street. I made it to my car, climbed in, waved, and then drove off quickly. I zigzagged for the next ten blocks to make sure no one was following me, all the while wondering how I could be so incredibly stupid.

Eventually, I crept back to the general area where the ice cream truck had been parked, but the street was clear. No vehicles anywhere, so I drove home at 3:15.

__Chapter Thirteen__

When I woke the next morning my neck was
stiff, my head throbbed and my side was killing me. I
figured it was because I'd slept on the couch and in my
clothes. Based on the empty fifth resting on the floor
I'd apparently poured myself a glass or two of Jameson
once I got home.

I groaned to my feet, took off my sport coat, and
made it to the bathroom. I stared back at the mirror in
disbelief at the purple bruise running the length of my
cheekbone. I lifted my polo shirt, saw another bruise
the size of a salad plate, and things started coming
together. Gradually, I remembered my stupid, stupid,
stupid attempt to place a bet at Mr. Swirlee's truck and
the run in with those goons in the street.

"You idiot," I sneered at the idiot staring back at
me in the bathroom mirror.

I had barely enough coffee in the cupboard to
make a pot and had just turned it on when the phone
rang. It took me a minute to find the damned thing
since it was still on the floor in my sport-coat pocket.

"Hello," I croaked, then cleared my throat.
"Hello," I managed with a little more authority.

"Well, how's it going this morning?"

It was the police. Actually, my pal Aaron LaZelle, a lieutenant with St. Paul's vice-squad. I'd known him since we'd been kids, and not just because he was on the vice-squad.

"Fine, if you don't go into detail," I replied, wishing the coffee to hurry up.

"Say, I have Detective Norris Manning in front of me just now."

I racked my brain, such as it was, but the name wasn't ringing a bell.

"Is that supposed to mean something to me? I'm not placing him. This isn't the guy we went ice fishing with, is it? The time that Janice chick…"

"No, this is a little more serious than that. Detective Manning finds you to be a person of interest. He spends most of his waking hours working homicide in this fair city and your name seems to have surfaced."

"Really?" I asked cautiously.

"It would be a good idea for you to pay a visit to our downtown office suite. Reacquaint yourself with some of our procedures and the responsibilities of upstanding citizens, such as yourself."

"Do I need a lawyer present?" I asked, getting very concerned.

"What time would you like him here?" I heard Aaron ask. Apparently Detective Manning really was in front of him.

"Sometime before noon would be fine," Aaron said to me. It was already twenty to eleven.

"Aaron, damn it, do I need a lawyer present?"

"I don't think so. Thank you for your cooperation. Ask for Detective Manning at the front desk. And make it soon. He's got a noon appointment."

"I'll have to make some calls, see if I can move a meeting around," I replied.

"Yeah, sure, you do that," he said, then hung up.

I ran through the events during the early morning hours at the ice cream truck. They were a bit hazy through the Jameson fog, but I couldn't come up with anything illegal. Well, except for the assault on me, and I wasn't pressing any charges.

I gingerly showered and shaved. Thought about using makeup or something on my face then decided that would only make things worse.

Chapter Fourteen

Aaron had mentioned that Detective Manning had a noon appointment. I arrived at eleven forty, calculating a ten-minute wait in the lobby, then five minutes to get to an interview room and five or ten minutes tops for questions. Not that I knew what Manning would be asking me.

"Oh, yeah, Mr. Haskell, I was alerted to your pending arrival." The desk sergeant chuckled when I explained why I was there.

Alerted to my pending arrival?

I found myself sitting in an interview room in about ninety seconds. The place smelled of sweat, cigarettes and fear. I thought the fear was from me.

"Ahhh, Mr. Haskell, is it? Good morning, thanks for coming in. I'm Detective Manning."

I guessed him to be about six two, maybe two hundred ten pounds, balding, red hair fringe, freckles, early forties, bright blue eyes, a hard charger. He looked a little like Terry Bradshaw and probably enjoyed a good joke. I didn't have any at the moment. He held a manila file under his left arm, carrying a machine-dispensed coffee cup in his left hand as he entered the interview room. He didn't offer to shake hands with me. His body language was telling me he was in charge, not that I needed a reminder.

"So," he said, sitting down.

I wanted to ask what this was about, but experience told me to shut up, answer precisely and with as few words as possible. I was pretty sure we were being watched through the one-way glass, probably Aaron, maybe a couple of other folks. Manning switched on a recorder, read the opening statement covering his ass, gave the date, time, my name, asked me if I was there of my own free will, then got down to business.

"Your name surfaced as a person of some interest in a matter under investigation. I'm hoping you'll be able to clear up some questions we have." He was doing what good investigators do, starting in generalities, suggesting the two of us could just work together to clear up a couple of items before I went on my way.

I was racking my brain, trying to figure out what this was about. The standoff last night? Pocketing a pair of diamond earrings I'd given an ex-girlfriend right before she dumped me? Letting a former girlfriend's parrot out the window last Memorial Day weekend? Stalking charges from that kindergarten teacher chick? President of the PMS club, Sandy from Connie Ortiz's office, about her DWI that I got pled down? Linda the...

"Mr. Haskell?"

"Oh, yeah, sorry. It's just that this is all so unexpected. Sorry, Detective, you were saying?"

Manning looked at me, and knew I'd broken the roll he was on. Knew I'd done it on purpose. The manila file lay open in front of him, and he took a long moment to read from the top sheet. Eventually he asked,

"Mr. Haskell, are you by any chance acquainted with a woman by the name of Lucille Lentz?"

I thought long and hard. I knew a lot of people, a lot of women, but Lucille Lentz was not one of them.

"No, I don't think I know anyone by that name. At least, not that I can remember at this time," I added, covering myself.

"I see." He turned a page, and read from the next sheet for a long minute.

"How about a man by the name of Harold Benton? Ever hear of him?"

"No, I don't think I know anyone by that name. At least that I can remember, at this time," I added again.

Manning looked up at me, smiled, stared for a moment then said, "Nice, you've done this once or twice before."

"Comes with the territory, I guess. I'm a private investigator."

"Yeah, we'll get to your job in just a moment," he said, turning the top sheet over and taking some time again to read from the next sheet.

"Have you ever heard of, or do you know a gentleman by the name of Monty Norling?"

"Norling?"

"Yes." Manning seemed to brighten just a bit.

"No, no idea who that might be. At least as far as I can recall."

He smiled again, but I wasn't sure he meant it.

"What about a man by the name of Willard B. Sneen?"

I thought for a moment. It was out there, but I wasn't connecting. I was beginning to regret at least the last two Jamesons I'd had before I fell asleep last night.

"No, I don't recall anyone by that name. At least to the best of my knowledge."

Manning smiled coldly.

"Nasty looking bruise on your face there. A fight? Trouble with someone's wife?" He half laughed.

"I'm not married," I replied, dodging.

"Oh, I'm sorry, maybe an ex girlfriend who filed a restraining order…"

"Which one do you have listed?"

"Which one?"

"Which ex girlfriend with the restraining order. I've had more than my share?"

"Bernice," he said, reading a name off some sort of bio sheet.

"No, she dumped me a couple of years back. You should have that in there, somewhere."

"You're right, we should," he said, turning a page and looking at the next sheet.

"Can you tell me where you were last night?"

"Last night?"

"Yes."

"I had a dinner meeting with clients, a contractual thing. I finished the meeting about nine thirty, met with some friends for a bit, then went home."

"What time did you get home?"

"Time?" I stalled. I couldn't believe those thugs had reported me. How did that work?

"Yes, what time did you arrive home?"

"I don't know, to tell you the truth. I wasn't really paying attention. I know I stayed up for a while. Had a couple of drinks, fell asleep on the couch."

"I see," Manning said, drumming his fingers on the tabletop, staring at me and maybe thinking.

"You see, Mr. Haskell, now I have a problem. We have witnesses who place you with someone last night. A number of witnesses as a matter of fact. We have a witness placing you with this same individual the day before. But you've told me you don't know this person. Yet you've met with him the past two days. Met him in out-of-the-way places. It's not exactly like running into someone walking down the street. Can you understand my problem? See, it becomes a coincidence for me, and as you might guess, I'm not all that fond of coincidences."

"Who the hell am I supposed to be meeting with? I didn't meet with anyone. Well, except some clients for dinner in their home last night?"

"You've stated you have no knowledge of Willard B. Sneen?"

"No, Willard…wait a minute…you mean Bernie? That fruitcake? Well, I mean I saw him last night, bought him a drink as a matter of fact. Not that he needed anymore. I saw him at The Spot. His name is Willard?"

"The Spot."

"Yeah, it's a little bar on the corner of Randolph and…"

"I'm familiar with The Spot, Mr. Haskell."

"Bernie's name is Willard? Like that old rat movie?"

Chapter Fifteen

The fact that Bernie's first name happened to be
Willard was the least of my problems. Turns out he'd
been found, or at least what was left of him, along the
railroad tracks after being hit by a freight train.

"We found your business card in Mr. Sneen's
pocket. We know you met with him earlier yesterday
evening and he was very upset when he left. We also
know you met him the day before and he departed that
meeting in a somewhat agitated state as well."

Manning was staring at me, unblinking. Those
once bright blue eyes now carried a decidedly icy cast.

"Look, I gave him my business card last night at
The Spot. He was hit by a freight train? What the hell?
I mean, he was sort of screwy, I guess. I just saw him
last night by accident. The day before, it was at
Dizzies, a bar over on…"

"We're familiar with the establishment."

"Okay, I knew he hung out there occasionally. I
wanted to talk with him about an investigation I'm
working on. He had some work experience in a
particular field and I wanted to learn more, that's all."

"Sneen had work experience?"

"Yes."

"Interesting, what's the investigation?"

"I'd have to claim client privilege there."

"All right."

"Do you know a woman by the name of Lucille Lentz?"

"I think you asked me that one before. No, I don't. To the best of my knowledge at this time," I added with a little smile.

"What about a gentleman by the name of Weldon Swirlmann?"

That wiped the smile off my face.

"Yeah, I mean, he's my client. He…"

"I see, but you don't know Lucille Lentz? His, I guess, what? Associate?"

"Lucille? You don't mean Lola? His wife? Nice looking blonde, pretty big…her name is Lucille?"

Not good, I thought.

"Tell me about Mr. Sneen getting upset last night. What did you say to him?"

"He was…well no offense, but the guy was somewhat unstable at the best of times, you know? And, he'd been drinking last night. He was telling me about some industrial accident he'd been involved in."

"Industrial accident?"

"Yeah, lost a finger."

"A finger?"

"Well, a couple, three, I guess. Course he never really got around to telling me exactly what happened. He just sort of went off the deep end. The poor guy started crying, then singing, bothering other customers, and they led him outside as kind of a nice way of kicking him out. That was the last I saw of him. Honest."

"This was when?"

"Probably about eleven, I would guess. I'm not sure exactly."

Manning paged back through a couple of sheets then made a note.

"And you left, when did you say?"

"I didn't say, actually. I think I closed the place."

"You think?"

"Kind of foggy on the latter part of the night."

"How did you get the bruise on your face?"

"I fell. At home," I added as an afterthought.

It went on like that for at least another hour. If Manning had a noon appointment, he was awfully late. I was regretting not grabbing a couple of Egg McMuffins or something to fill my stomach. Eventually, he wound things up.

"I guess that's all for right now, Mr. Haskell. I appreciate your help, here. We'll be in touch."

"That's it?"

"It is. For the time being, you're free to go."

I didn't argue.

Manning's little interview had done nothing to improve my hangover. I needed a drink. I kept a bottle of Maalox in the glove compartment of the Lincoln and chugged down a couple of healthy glugs as soon as I climbed in, then sat for some time, head pounding, while I attempted to think.

The odds were fifty-fifty Bernie threw himself in front of a freight train as opposed to being pushed. Manning had suggested Mr. Swirlee was involved. Of course, the way things were going, he might have thought I could have done Bernie in, too. Hopefully, the same witnesses who told him about Bernie also confirmed I closed up The Spot last night. I figured if I really needed more witnesses I could always try and track down the thugs who beat me up, or the bald prick who threatened to splatter me across the street with his shotgun. I was sure they'd be willing to help.

There was someone else I could check with, too.

Chapter Sixteen

I was a half block away from the old gas station where the Giant Scoop office was located when I spotted a large pile of rubble out in front of the building. The moment I opened the door of my car I could smell smoke, wet plaster, and something like bad milk from my refrigerator. The two Giant Scoop ice cream trucks were parked in their bays and now just charred hulks.

Jill stood out front, talking to a couple of guys in yellow hard hats and white hazmat suits. SPFD was emblazoned across their shoulders in large red letters, Saint Paul Fire Department. A Channel Five news van was just pulling around the corner. I stood off to the side for a few more minutes while Jill finished her conversation. At one point she looked over and saw me, but didn't acknowledge the fact. Eventually, they all shook hands and the two guys walked over to a fire department SUV parked at the curb.

Jill stood with her back to me. One foot was planted in a small stream of water oozing from the pile of rubble, and running across the concrete apron and into the street.

I waited a moment before I approached.

"Jill, are you okay? What happened here?"

She turned and looked at me with a tearstained face, but her jaw was set firm and her eyes flashed fire.

"Get the fuck out of my sight," she said slowly, a razor edge on every word.

"Look, Jill, I don't know anything about any of this. Honest. I...I just came from the police station, dealing with something else. What...what happened?"

"Like you don't know."

"Really, I don't, I don't have any idea."

"Who else but your pal, that asshole, Mr. Swirlee. What? We weren't losing money fast enough for his taste?"

"Look, first of all, he's not my pal. Okay? Secondly, I...well, I don't know what to say. Tell me what I can do to help in some way."

"You? Help?"

"Yeah, if I can. First of all, tell me what happened here."

"What happened is someone fire-bombed us last night. Those two guys are arson investigators." She nodded at the SUV pulling away from the curb. "They're going to file their report saying we were fire-bombed. It'll slow down any insurance payment for a couple of years."

"What?"

"Yeah, they already warned me. They'll try and claim it was us. The insurance company, that is. You know, they're your best friend until you really need them. We've never missed a payment in something like forty-seven years and suddenly we're gonna be the bad guys. I just know it, goddamn it." She shuddered then looked the other way and wiped the tears from her cheeks. I could see her shoulders shaking as she fought to keep everything together.

I'm not necessarily a caring, sensitive type of guy, but I automatically stepped closer and wrapped my arms around her. She broke into deep sobs, crying for a long minute.

"Grandpa, grandpa, I'm so sorry," she sobbed. Eventually she came to her senses.

"Let go of me, you creep." She sniffled and then shook her way out of my embrace.

Past experience had taught me not to argue.

"Look, Jill, I'm really sorry. But I don't know anything about…"

"Just go, will you? Things are bad enough without you being here."

I thought that was probably a pretty good idea, and so I left.

Chapter Seventeen

I stood listening to the ringing on the other end of the line. Either no one was home at Mr. Swirlee's or they were ignoring me. The dogs were lying on the front steps, just resting. No doubt they were conserving their energy until the next innocent was buzzed through the front gate. I was in no mood for their routine and planned to tell Mr. Swirlee as soon as someone answered, but at the rate things were going that was liable to be tomorrow. I hung up and dialed again. Someone picked up on the second ring.

"Yes?" It was either Lola or a child from a nearby kindergarten.

"Hi, Lola. Dev Haskell."

"Dev?" she asked, sounding more like she had no idea.

"Yeah, the investigator. I was here last night. You signed a contract. Remember?"

"Contract?"

Suddenly there was a buzz, and the lock on the gate clicked open.

Heads shot up on the two evil dogs sitting on the front steps. They held their position, but I could tell they were waiting for the gate to swing open. One of them licked his snout.

I dialed the phone again. It rang interminably. Eventually the front door opened, and Lola stood in the doorway.

"It's the dogs. Could you put them away?" I called.

Their growls began to rumble across the lawn.

She looked at me for a moment, as if she were translating, then clapped her hands and said,

"Come on, come on, puppies, let's go." They followed her inside, tail stubs wagging.

Puppies? I waited a few moments before I pushed the gate open, then walked to the open front door. Lola stood in the hallway,

"Come on, he's in the study," she called like she had been waiting for me all day. She motioned me forward. She was wearing a very, very short black skirt, some sort of spaghetti-strap black top and a wide red belt.

I could hear scratching and growling coming from the rear of the house, back toward the kitchen, if memory served. I prayed the door held.

Mr. Swirlee sat slumped behind his desk in a large black leather chair, the ever-present cell phone attached to his ear. His walker was pushed off to the side. He was nodding repeatedly at a voice on the other end. Eventually, he snarled by way of acknowledgment and hung up.

"Looking a little worse for the wear. What happened to you?" he said, noticing my bruised face.

"Industrial accident, helping a friend clean up after a fire."

He didn't blink.

"What have you got for me? And don't tell me nothing!"

"Actually something has surfaced," I said.

"Oh?" He creaked the black leather chair forward, eyes riveted on me.

Lola shifted from one foot to the other, and then back again, she crossed her arms, bit her lower lip and maybe looked just a little wide eyed.

"Yeah, I'm picking up reports of a disgruntled employee. He sounds a little unstable."

"Christ, that could be just about any one of them." Swirlee shook his head.

"This guy seems to have made some threats. At least, he threatened to harm you in some way."

"Not much help. It could still be just about anyone I know," he said.

Lola nodded in agreement.

I wasn't going to argue.

"You remember one of your ice cream truck drivers from awhile back, last name Sneen?" I was looking for some sort of reaction.

Lola may have shot a quick glance at Mr. Swirlee, maybe not. I wasn't sure.

"Sneen is the last name? Can't say I remember anyone named Sneen, but there's so damned much turnover with those bastards. What makes you think he might be the one?"

"Claims he was assaulted or something. I'm still checking that part out although he seems to have gone missing all of a sudden. I was planning to follow him around, see what I might learn."

"And now you can't find the bastard. I'm not surprised. Hell, he's probably up in the tree out front with a high-powered rifle and a sniper scope. Wonderful! Just great!"

"No, I checked the tree."

"What did he say we did?" Lola asked.

"As near as I can determine he claims he was wrongfully discharged for stealing funds." I sugarcoated Bernie's version.

"Wrongfully discharged?" Mr. Swirlee chuckled. "Bastard was stealing from me. I remember now, he was pilfering cash. I think he had some sort of chemical problem, nervous little son-of-a-bitch. We attempted some sort of rehabilitation, if memory serves. Yeah, definitely the unstable sort."

Lola nodded in agreement.

"Rehabilitation." It was my turn to chuckle.

"You know how these people are," Lola said.

"Idiots, thieves, dregs of society," Mr. Swirlee added.

"So you think he's the one who crashed into us the other night?" Lola asked.

"I think it's entirely possible. I'd like to check out a few more leads I have, see what I can come up with. Nail down his whereabouts, type of vehicle he drives, that sort of thing."

"That won't be necessary. He's our man. I'll handle it from here," Mr. Swirlee said, then picked up his phone and punched in a number.

"Well, in all honesty, Sneen looks like a good candidate, but there are a lot of other people who don't think all that kindly of you."

"You don't get to be a man like me without stepping on a few toes along the way. No, that'll be all. I'll handle things from here. Just send me your bill so I can get this off my desk. I got a lot of things about to happen."

"The bill? Look, you only signed up last night, less than eighteen hours ago. I really think it might be wise if I..."

"What part of no don't you understand? Hello. Carl, hang on a minute," he said into the phone. Then looked over at Lola and nodded.

"Let me show you out," she squeaked, sounding only too happy to do so.

"Carl," Mr. Swirlee shouted as he spun around in his chair to face out the window.

I followed Lola back down the hallway toward the front door. She was taking little steps again, this time due to a pair of black, sling-back stiletto heels, some sort of red flames emblazoned across the toes and up the sides, the perfect outfit to lounge around the house.

"Gee, really sorry we couldn't do more together," she said at the front door. Then smiled and gave another of her patented shrugs. "Bye-bye." She giggled and hustled me out, closing the door before I had a chance to say anything. I heard the door lock behind me.

Fortunately, my luck seemed to hold and the dogs were still inside. I made my way quickly to the gate, but not before glancing at the front steps. There, chewed almost in half, was a black high-top shoe, faded almost to grey, with a red shoelace. Cheap. It looked an awful lot like one Bernie Sneen was wearing the day I saw him at Dizzies. Just as I approached the gate I heard a buzz and the electronic click released the lock. A moment later the front door opened and the dogs were out.

Chapter Eighteen

I mailed my bill to Mr. Swirlee that afternoon. I spent the next three days working on the phone, attempting to confirm resume facts for a legal firm. It was dull work, but allowed me to sleep late, wear sweatpants, drink a few beers, and overcharge my client. I'd been doing just that, drinking beer, wearing sweatpants and in general being worthless when the phone rang waking me up.

"Yello." Was how it came out, I had a beer burp at the same time.

"Oh, I think I might have the wrong number. I was trying to reach Haskell Investigations," a female voice said.

"You got me," I replied, coming awake and stretching on the couch. It was about two in the afternoon and researching statements on resumes had lost its luster days earlier.

"Dev?"

"Yeah, who's this?"

"Jill. Jill Lydell."

It took me a moment. I'd never gotten her last name and the send off she'd given me in front of the

77

Giant Scoop after the fire hadn't left me with a lot of hope for future contact.

"Oh yeah, Jill. Nice to hear from you. How are things going?"

"Okay, I guess. You know, everything considered. I was wondering if maybe we could get together and…first of all I wanted to say I'm really, really sorry for the way I act…"

"Forget it you were a lot better than I could ever hope to be under the circumstances. Just for the record, I'm not working for Mr. Swirlee. I had a contract with the guy that didn't last twenty-four hours."

"No surprise there," she said.

"Look, I'd love to get together. I'm finishing up an investigation right now," I said, placing a can of warm beer on the floor and sitting up on the couch.

"What's your schedule like?" she asked.

"Schedule? Well, nothing I can't adjust. What did you have in mind?"

"The sooner the better. Would tonight work?"

"It could. You tell me where and when. I'll rearrange things."

"Well, tonight, if that's not too soon. You know the Sportsman's Bar?"

"I do."

I'd been kicked out of there years back for being underage.

"Say seven-thirty?"

"See you there."

Chapter Nineteen

I was on time for a change, and Jill was waiting for me in a back booth looking a lot better than the last time I saw her.

She waved as I approached. She tilted her head so I could kiss her cheek, and I caught a hint of her perfume…nice.

"Thanks for coming. Get you something?" she asked. A waitress was right on my heels.

"Leinenkugel for me," I said and looked over at Jill.

"I'll have another one of these." She held out a glass which looked like a Coke.

"Okay, so tell me where you're at. What are your plans with the business?" I asked.

"Well, everyone has been really great. The neighborhood is holding a fundraiser for us next Saturday. You oughta come. Obviously, the biggest thing is getting some new vehicles, but they are so expensive. We'll just have to see. To tell you the truth, it's looking like the rest of this year might be an absolute wash. I mean, once it gets cold, you can forget about sales, you know? We're doing a stand at the Farmer's Market. They let us in ahead of all sorts of people because of the fire. It's going okay, but it's only Saturday and Sunday. Still, every little bit helps."

"Any word from your insurance company? You were a little worried about them when we talked."

"Yeah, look, I want to apologize. I was really upset and…"

"No need. I get it. Like I said, I think you handled things a lot better than I would have done."

When our drinks arrived, I took a long sip while Jill continued.

"Yeah, but you got my explosion and you didn't deserve it. You said on the phone you're not working for Mr. Swirlee anymore?"

I shook my head in disgust.

"No, man, imagine one of my clients acting strange. Go figure. They signed a contract with me one night, then said they didn't need me the following afternoon. I wasn't even on the payroll for twenty-four hours."

"You might have gotten off lucky," she said.

"By the way, I was working on something completely unrelated to your situation. To be honest, he thought someone tried to kill him. I think it was a simple hit-and-run. Along the way I learned you'd have to rent Carnegie Hall to hold all the people who don't like the guy."

"Yeah, well, you can still count Annie and me on your list." She took a sip. "Not because we tried to do anything," she added quickly.

"Not to worry. Like I said, I'm off the case. Now, I just have to get paid."

"Lots of luck."

"I sent him my bill."

She looked at me with a slight smile.

"He's one of those people who figures since he doesn't owe you much, you'll only go so far in pursuing it. So if he just sits tight and doesn't pay, he figures eventually you'll just throw up your hands and write it off," she said.

"He would be mistaken. Look, let's not ruin the evening talking about creeps. You mentioned you had something you wanted me to look into."

"Well, yeah. The fire."

"Okay."

"See, I got this call from someone across the street. A house full of college girls, they rent. Anyway, they had a party, the thing begins to wind down about four in the morning. One of the girls goes to bed, she looks out the window, and there's two guys outside of the Giant Scoop."

"Yeah?" I said, waiting for the real information.

"Well, then a little later the fire happened. At first she didn't think much of it, but when she heard the news report saying arson was suspected, she phoned me."

"Did she phone the cops?"

"I asked her to. I don't know if she did or not."

"I see," I said, thinking this was really slim, but I didn't want to sound discouraging.

"So, doesn't it sound like a real clue or something?"

"Yes, it does," I said, thinking two guys at four in the morning. What were the odds they just stopped to take a piss.

"So, now what do I say? Something like, will you take the case?"

"I'll check it out for you, Jill. But I can't promise anything. Do you know this woman's name?"

She reached into her purse and handed me a slip of paper.

"Jennifer McCauley. She's a student at the U. Here's her address and phone number. I think she's a waitress, works nights. But I told her someone might call her, so she's sort of expecting it...you know, your call."

"I'll check it out," I said.

"What's this gonna cost me?"

"How about you just let me check this out and we'll see what develops. Okay?"

"I don't want to be a charity case," she said with that sharp edge back in her voice.

"You're not. Hey, don't shoot me for trying to do you a favor. I can be a nice guy, once in a while. Look, let me check into this, see if anything turns up. If it looks like there's something there, then we can start talking about my modest expenses. Fair?"

"Yeah, sorry I snapped. That's fair. As long as you let me buy dinner," she said.

"No argument. I'll start with another Leinenkugel."

Chapter Twenty

Jennifer McCauley was a waitress at a place down on West Seventh called Shamrock's, not far from The Spot. She had dark curly hair, big brown eyes, a nice figure, and a twenty-something sense about her suggesting she was completely unaware of how the world worked.

We sat at the bar and talked once she finished her shift.

"Oh, my, God! You really are, like, a private investigator? That is so awesome," she said, reading the business card I had just handed her, then looked up wide eyed.

Just to keep up the professional impression I'd pulled on a relatively clean polo shirt, a sport coat, and pressed jeans.

"Like, do you arrest creeps for murder, chase kidnappers, and things like that? You know, like the CSI guys and stuff." She took a healthy sip of her Captain and Coke then stared.

"Not all the time," I said.

"Awesome."

"First of all, Jennifer, thanks for calling Jill Lydell about the guys you saw in front of her place. Did you ever file a report with the police?"

"A report?"

"Yeah, it's always a good idea to call them, let them know what you saw."

"Oh, well, I guess I sort of forgot to do that. Kind of busy here and all, you know?"

"Yeah, I can imagine it gets pretty crazy waitressing from six till ten. Tell me what you told Jill."

"Well, it really wasn't much, you know? Least I didn't think so at first, but then once I saw the news story about it being arson, I thought I should call her."

I nodded like I was following.

"So you called her?"

"Yeah." She smiled a large smile, nodded enthusiastically and took another big gulp of her Captain and Coke.

"And what did you tell her?" I prodded.

"Jill?"

"Yes, Jill. What did you tell her, when you called?" I was trying to cover all the bases.

"Just that I saw two guys out there in front. I don't know how long they'd been there. I think I was getting ready for bed."

"What time was this?" I asked, hoping to keep her thought process moving.

"It was probably a little after like four, I think. I can't really be sure because...well, you know, the party that night."

"So a little after four, you see these guys in front of the Giant Scoop. What were they doing?"

"Actually, they were watching me. I don't have air conditioning in my room, so the windows are open, you know? And I guess they were watching me get undressed." She stated it as a casual fact, like it didn't seem to bother her.

"They were in a car?"

"Yeah. Well, actually, not in it. The car was parked in front of the Scoop. That's what we call the place, the Scoop. Anyway, it was parked, you know, like it was going to drive into one of the parking places in front of the building. Only the doors were closed."

"So they were pulled in front of the garage doors?"

She seemed to think for half a moment, drained some more from her drink, and then nodded.

"Yeah, yeah, like they were ready to pull the door up and just drive in. Only they didn't."

"Can you describe them, what they looked like?"

"Well, they were both sort of big guys, you know? Not fat, exactly. More like muscle guys."

"Did they look like basketball players or bodybuilders?"

"Kinda more the bodybuilder type, not skinny like I think of a basketball player."

"Were they wearing anything special that might make them stand out? Maybe a certain baseball cap or possibly a shirt with something written on it?"

"No, no, nothing like that. I think just jeans and, you know, T-shirts, I think. But it was sort of too dark to really see them. I think one of the guys was bald, I remember that. Oh, yeah, and the other one wore glasses, now that I think about it."

"The guy with glasses, did he have long hair?"

"Oh, wow, I'm sorry. I just can't remember."

"What sort of vehicle did they have?"

The bartender arrived and automatically stiffened her drink with a healthy pour from the Captain Morgan bottle.

"It was big, some kind of like SUV. I think it was sort of white, shiny. I can't really remember. I mean, I wasn't paying that close attention. They were looking at me and I didn't have anything on, so I stared back, then just turned out the light and climbed into bed. I was asleep before my head hit the pillow."

"Okay, so then, did you wake up with the explosion?"

"Well, no, not really. I guess I sort of slept through all that."

"Did you wake up when the fire trucks arrived? You know, the sirens, lights, and all the smoke and flames?"

"Yeah, see, I guess I sort of missed that part, too," she said, looking like she was trying very hard to think.

"So, when did you learn about the fire?"

"Oh, when I came to work that evening, here. I mean, I leave home out the back door, so I never saw all the junk out in front of the Scoop. You know, all the burnt shit piled up. It was on the news, and I was watching, thinking that place sure looks familiar and all. I mean, you know, we'd had that party the night before so..."

"Actually, not surprisingly, I do know how that works when you've had a party. So two guys who looked like bodybuilder types, one bald, one with glasses and a white SUV. Anything else?"

"Nothing I can really remember. Oh, one thing, the lights were really bright."

"The lights?"

"Yeah, you know, on their car. Those really bright kind of headlights, sort of almost looking blue. They were shining against the windows in the garage doors. On the Scoop building, you know, reflecting like."

I nodded.

"Hey, can I hang onto this card and show my friends? They'll think it's really cool."

"Yeah, sure, you bet. Here, pass these around," I said, pulling a half dozen out of my wallet and handing them to her.

"Oh, wow, thanks. They are gonna freak."

We parted. Jennifer was getting another rum top-up on her Captain and Coke as I left. I fled to the sanity of The Spot. Thinking on the way, two muscle-bound guys, a white SUV. It sounded an awful lot like the charmers I met trying to place a bet at 2:30 in the morning. Had those guys grabbed Bernie Sneen, then fire-bombed the Giant Scoop? Busy night.

Chapter Twenty-One

The next morning I called Aaron LaZelle, my vice-squad pal. I left a message. He phoned me back before I was through with my second cup of coffee.

"You're up early," he said.

I glanced at the clock on my microwave. 10:57.

"Yeah, well, you know the early worm gets the bird."

"What can I do for you?"

"Willard Sneen," I said.

"You mean Bernie?"

"Yeah, tell that to your homicide pal, Manning."

"What about him? Bernie, I mean?"

"Other than being hit by a train, was there anything else unusual?"

"Since you remain a person of interest I would tell you that you are skittering around the edges of privileged information right about now. However, your question suggests that, despite your lackadaisical nature, you have managed to stumble across some tidbit of information which could be of interest to us. At which point, I would advise you to contact Detective Norris Manning, directly. Then you can relay whatever modest fact you might have acquired."

"So you don't know anything?"

"To tell you the truth, I don't. In case you haven't heard we are still in the throes of massive budget cuts due to the great recession. Prostitution and gambling, two things near and dear to my heart, have 'F'ing skyrocketed, and we have zero resources just now. So, unless your pal Bernie was with a call girl and placing a bet when the freight train took him out, I got other fish to fry. Call Manning."

"I'm not sure he likes me."

"Of course he doesn't. Who can blame him? No one likes you. Look, give him a call. Like all of us, he's got a full plate. Any help you can offer would be appreciated."

"Well, I wonder if you could just find out if…"

"No. I don't have time to screw around with your bullshit. Anything else?"

"Yeah, it's your turn to buy dinner."

"I'll get back to you on that one. Bye."

I phoned Jill next.

"Hi, Dev. What's up?"

"Did you ever get a report from your arson-investigator pals?"

"Yeah, almost immediately, as a matter of fact. I sent it off to the insurance company. I've got a copy here in my office."

"Your office? I thought everything was destroyed."

"It was. Right now the office is my dining room table. I could let you see it if you think it would help, but I don't want it going too far out of my hands. It's about all we've got right now."

"Could I swing by later today?"

"Anytime. Not like I'm busy or anything. I gotta run some errands in a bit. Look, could you make it for dinner?"

"Thanks, but I don't want to impose," I said, sounding disingenuous.

"I'll see you at seven, bring a bottle of wine. White. You're having chicken tonight."

Chapter Twenty-Two

I thought about my conversation with Aaron. I had the feeling there was more to Bernie Sneen's death than some drunk staggering along the railroad tracks. The little bit of information from Jennifer McCauley was nagging in the back of my mind. Eventually, I placed a call to Detective Manning and left a message.

Manning returned my call maybe forty-five minutes later. I was asleep on the couch when the phone rang.

"Detective Manning, returning your call."

"Thanks for calling back, Detective," I said, trying to wake up and sound helpful at the same time.

"What can I do for you?"

"I wonder if we could meet, maybe away from your office. I have some questions."

"You have questions? Interesting. I'm awfully busy. I really don't have that kind of time, but I'm down here in my office the rest of the afternoon if you wanted to add anything to your statement."

"You ever grab coffee in the morning?"

"Possibly."

"I'll be at Nina's, Selby and Western, tomorrow morning."

"How early?" he asked.

"You name it," I said.

"Seven."

He was yanking my chain. Seven in the damn morning was a lot earlier than I had planned.

"I'll be there," I said, hiding my disgust at the early hour.

Chapter Twenty-Three

Trying to think positive on a hot evening, I showed up at Jill's with two bottles of chilled wine. She hadn't been kidding on her location. She was directly across the alley from the now boarded-up Giant Scoop building.

Her home was a neatly kept, Cape Cod-style house with a redbrick front, two dormers on the second floor, and dark green siding with gold trim. I guessed it had been built about 1948.

"There you are," she said at the front door. She was barefoot, wearing white shorts and a pink T-Shirt with the Giant Scoop logo across the front. She gave me a peck on the cheek then relieved me of both bottles of wine.

"God, who have you been talking to?" She laughed.

"What?"

"Lucky guess," she said, but didn't comment further.

I followed her into a comfortable kitchen. She picked up a platter with chicken breasts marinating in something dark from the kitchen counter.

"Wine glasses are in that cupboard." She nodded. "Open one of those and pour me a glass, please. Then, if you could put the wine in the fridge. Oh, help yourself to a beer if you'd prefer."

I handed her the wine glass. Condensation was already dripping down the sides. We walked out the back door onto a very nice deck. The backyard sloped gradually down toward the alley. Well-tended flower gardens ran along three sides of the yard. A rear gate with an arbor way opened to the alley. Some sort of vine thing with pink flowers wound around the arbor. I knew it wasn't a rose, but didn't know much more than that

"Oh, God I need this. What a day," she said after a healthy swallow.

"I'll bet. It looks like you're never very far from work." I nodded toward the Giant Scoop building across the alley. Other than the plywood over the windows and rear door there was no real outward sign of damage in the back.

"Yeah, well, I was raised in this house. That place was always there. I think I started working at about age five."

"Five." I chuckled.

"Really. I would go over there and help my grandpa count stock, arrange the boxes. I was a good little worker."

"I bet you were. And you just stayed with it?"

"Yeah, more or less. You know, went away to college, the U...accounting, if you're wondering. A marriage that failed after a few years and here I am with a boarded-up building over there representing thirty-plus years of my life. Thank God this place is paid for," she said, looking around the yard, then washed her statement down with some more wine.

"Yeah. Hey, I talked with Jennifer, the waitress."

"What'd you think?"

"About her? I think she's like a lot of kids. Seems nice enough. Works just enough to pay the rent, parties, tans, and right now doesn't have to take life too seriously. She's cute and has a lot of guys more than happy to buy her drinks."

She took another sip. "I meant, what did you think about what she saw?"

"Well, it could just be two guys going home who glanced up and then hung around to watch the show. Apparently, she was getting ready for bed and hadn't drawn the shade. So it's a possibility. There are a couple of things kind of odd, though. Their vehicle was pulled in front of one of the garage doors, and they were out of the vehicle. I don't know, they could have been checking their tires. They could have been trying to get a better view of Jennifer. Or, they could have been setting a fire. It's one of the reasons I wanted to read your copy of the arson report. They'll have some more details. Not the least of which is where the blaze started."

"Just inside the west door. I already read the report. Think it means something?"

"Where the fire started?"

"Yeah."

"It definitely means something. I just don't know what exactly yet. The two guys not being involved is sounding pretty slim. They just happen to be there innocently, at four in the morning, then sometime later someone else wanders by and sets the fire. I doubt it."

We continued to chat through a pleasant dinner on her deck. I helped carry the dishes back into the kitchen.

"Oh, thanks. Anything left in that bottle of wine?" She looked hopeful.

"It's empty, but there's a second one."

She studied me for just a moment.

"I shouldn't," she said and held out her glass.

"You're right, you shouldn't, but you might as well because I'm going to sit down and read the arson report and you'll be bored."

"You talked me into it."

As reports go it was clinical. Which was fine with me. I read through it, then reread the pertinent sections twice more. Cut down to the basic facts, the fire had been set using a small butane tank and a little timing device held in place with duct tape. Remnants of a tank consistent with the type used in a small camping stove had been recovered on site. The device had been placed in close proximity to flammable substances that served as additional accelerant, blah, blah, blah.

In other words, someone crammed this thing next to gas and turpentine cans stored close to the door, set it to go off, and ran.

Jill sat in her living room, watching back to back episodes of Sex in the City and sipping wine. She'd gotten up twice to refill her glass and carried the bottle back in with her the last time. She was curled up on the corner of the couch, looking very lovely.

"Good show?" I asked getting up from her dining-room table.

"You kidding? Sex in the City. I love it."

"Is this the one where Charlotte pisses off Miranda, Miranda gets kind of bitchy, Samantha has weird sex with a young guy, and Carrie screws up her date with Mr. Big?"

"You've seen this one?" she asked, surprised.

"No, just a wild guess."

"Come here and watch it with me," she said, patting the cushion next to her, then taking a sip of wine.

The offer was very tempting.

"Thanks, but I better not. I've got an early morning meeting."

"Really? Afraid to mix business with pleasure? Or are you just playing hard to get?" she asked, then sipped some more, staring at me over the rim of her glass.

The bottle on the coffee table was empty. Being a guy, I made a mental note after calculating her drinks consumed to frisky ratio.

"No, really, I do have a meeting. As a matter of fact, I'm talking with a detective on some aspects of the fire and I wanna be sharp. So, if I could take a rain check?"

"Okay, your loss."

"I don't doubt it, but I better not. Thanks for dinner, I really enjoyed it. I'll keep you posted."

She set her glass down on the coffee table, maybe just a little too heavily, then got up and walked toward the front door.

"Okay, you'll call me tomorrow? After your meeting?"

"I'll call you."

She stepped up, gave me a long kiss, then followed me aggressively with her tongue for a half moment as I attempted to pull away.

"Thanks." She grinned, then opened the door, and stood partially blocking the way so I had to brush past her. "Enjoy the rest of the night." She laughed as I walked toward my car.

Chapter Twenty-Four

Nina's Coffee Shop, at the corner of Selby and Western, sits in the shadow of the Cathedral and almost within sight of my front door. It's one of the very few beverage establishments I frequent that does not dispense alcohol. At seven in the morning a constant stream of customers come in the front door and line up to place orders. Upwards of thirty people were seated around the place, conversing and tapping keys on laptops. Everyone seemed just a little too perky and positive for my early morning taste.

Twenty minutes later, Detective Norris Manning walked in, nodded, and then took his place in line. He ordered a large latte, two large caramel-slathered pastries, and pointed at me when it came time to pay.

I nodded at June, the owner, who just rolled her eyes.

"Thanks." Manning slurped his latte as he sat down across from me.

"My pleasure," I lied.

He wore a dark suit, and as he sat down I caught the briefest glimpse of a black leather shoulder holster. A waft of aftershave drifted in with him. The top of his bald head was a decided pink from a recent shower.

His tie was loosened, and the top button of his white shirt was undone.

"Face seems to have healed up," he said, studying at me.

"Thank you. I wasn't aware you cared so much."

"So, what have you got for me?" he asked, then crammed more than half a pastry into his mouth. He proceeded to noisily and purposefully lick caramel from the tips of his fingers.

"Good?" I asked as he sucked his little finger just a moment longer.

"The best." He smiled.

"I had a question on the Willard B. Sneen case."

"You mean Bernie?" he asked.

"Yeah, Bernie. Do you guys have any theories? I mean, are you thinking suicide, a drunken accident, or murder?"

"Actually, it's still an ongoing investigation. Why do you ask?" He stuffed the remainder of his first pastry into his mouth. Then smiled at me like a kid on Halloween night.

"Hey look, Manning, I know you spoke with Aaron LaZelle. You know we're friends, he and I. I may have come across something that would help. I don't know. I do know this…it's early in the morning for me and I don't need to play games. I do know when I last saw Bernie he was not stable. He was intoxicated, may have been on drugs as well, and seemed at best to be agitated. Not a good mix. I also know, or at least think, Bernie would not take his own life."

"What makes you think so?"

"Nothing specific, just a general sense. Was the guy nutty? Absolutely. A drunk? Yeah. Drugs? Most likely. Did he seem to be harboring some sort of darkness and it might get the better of him? I don't think so. From what I hear he'd been a mess most of his life, never really done anything other than screw up. I'm just not sure there was anything that could have set him off, or push him over the edge and into the deep end."

Manning nodded, seemed to think about it as he tore off a relative dainty third of the remaining pastry and tossed it into his mouth.

"He was pretty bombed when they led him out. The nearest train tracks are about a mile from The Spot. I'm not sure he could have made it, at least, not on his own. Can you guys check and see what the train schedule is? Maybe that would…"

"Nice thinking, master sleuth. You know, occasionally we do check on things. He was hit at approximately 11:57. By the way, I'm guessing you think this was probably over around Sheppard Road and Randolph, right?"

"That's the most likely train crossing. It's in the general direction of the rooming house where he lived. 'Course there's another one over…"

"Actually, he was found in the switching yard, just east of downtown."

"The switching yard? About five miles away? And he's on foot? I know he couldn't have made it, even if he was sober he wouldn't have been able to go that far, especially in just under an hour. The guy couldn't run a block, let alone five miles."

"Especially barefoot and all wrapped up in duct tape the way he was."

"Duct tape?"

"Yeah, over his mouth, around his legs, his wrists. Someone wrapped him up like a rug then laid him across the tracks. He'd been punched a couple of times, pretty hard. Had a real nasty dog bite on his ass. It's why I was interested in the bruise you were sporting when you came in for your interview. But, there are a number of barflies attesting to the fact you were in The Spot until they threw you out sometime after closing. A couple of hours after your pal Bernie caught it."

"Jesus."

"No, Jesus must have been busy." Manning smiled at his joke. "Based on what was left of him, we're guessing he had some idea of what was going on. The theory is he tried to roll into the center of the tracks, hoping the freight would just pass over him. I'd say his plan didn't work too well."

"Suspects?"

"Besides you? The usual. It wouldn't be uncommon to have a murder like this over a fifteen-dollar debt or a half pint. There's always that a certain element, the puddle of slime oozing around the ladder of society. It's been almost a week now, with no real leads. This could well be a cold case in pretty short order. Not that I won't keep working the damn thing."

"What about Swirlmann?" I asked.

"Mr. Swirlee? He's slippery, but I don't figure him for this. He may have a finger in a lot of things, but killing some lowlife like your pal Bernie…I don't think so."

"He used to work for Swirlee."

"Yeah, we checked, it was a couple of years back. They fired his ass for stealing. I think he was one of four guys let go that season. We checked their records. Seems to come with the territory. Swirlee usually hires college kids, but come mid-August they're all heading back to school. So, they hire folks who shouldn't be anywhere near kids, Sneen being one of them." He licked more caramel off his fingers.

"Besides, Swirlee was confined to bed. He broke his leg or ankle in some sort of fall before this deal went down."

"Did you check that out?"

"Who are you, internal affairs? Yeah, as a matter of fact, we did check it out. He was hospitalized. The nurses remembered him because he was such a pain in the ass." He slurped more latte and glared at me over his cup.

"I don't know," I said absently.

"Probably the only correct thing you've said. What? You think you got something to add that might help?" he scoffed.

"Nothing you don't already know. I was trying to put together the distance to the train tracks and how screwed up Bernie was at the time. But, I guess I was way off base to begin with. I didn't know about the duct tape and him being hit way over in the switching yard."

"Yeah, we're keeping it quiet," he said, then crammed the remainder of the sticky pastry into his mouth, and slurped the last of his latte.

"Detective, thanks for setting me straight."

"Always a pleasure, Haskell. Call me if you'd ever like me to do it again. Don't forget to settle up before you leave," he said. He pushed his chair in, then gave me a little wink and walked out the door.

I sat thinking of the shoe Swirlee's dog was chewing a few days back. Poor Bernie, barefoot, bitten and wrapped in duct tape with a freight train barreling down on him, no one deserved that. Not a very happy thought.

Chapter Twenty-Five

It was a little past noon. Another cloudless, scorching sky. The day was hot, muggy, and held the promise of getting much worse. I decided to pay a courtesy call on my former client.

As usual I cooled my heels while the phone at the front gate rang and rang. Eventually Lola picked up.

"Yes?"

"Hi, Lola, Dev Haskell. Sorry to drop by unannounced, but I was wondering if I might steal a minute or two of your time." I really wasn't sorry.

"I'd love it," she said, and the gate lock snapped open almost immediately.

"Any worry about the dogs?" I asked, peeking around the yard, expecting the things to lunge out at any moment. Amazingly, she was still on the line.

"No, they're out getting a bath and their nails done. They'll be gone for hours. Come on in," she said, and snapped the lock again.

Just as I got to the front steps she opened the door, and stood in the entry. She was wearing a very small bikini, a very large smile and sipping from a martini glass. Nice work if you can get it.

"You're just in time. I was getting ready to work on my tan. Come on, this will be fun. Close the door behind you." She sauntered down the hall toward the rear of the house. Her bikini bottom was a thong, a very small powder blue thong, to go with her extremely small, powder blue top.

I had the sense of complete emptiness. Other than her heels clicking down the hallway as she walked, the only other sound was the clock ticking when we passed Mr. Swirlee's office. The lights were off in the room and I noticed the hospital bed was gone. I couldn't see his walker.

Lola strutted across the kitchen, opened the freezer door, and refilled her glass from a frosted pitcher. She took a deep sip, then topped the glass off and returned the pitcher to the freezer.

"Delicious." She grinned, raising her eyebrows.

I waited in vain for the offer of a cold beer.

"Come on," she turned and headed out the patio door.

The back yard was picture-postcard beautiful, not so much as a blade of grass out of place. Music was playing from somewhere, pure crap. I couldn't tell who the band was, but I knew I didn't like them. There was a cushioned lawn chair stretched out on the patio, covered with a long beach towel sporting blue stripes to match her thong. A pillow rested at one end. A small round end table, metal with a granite top, stood close to the pillow. A tube of suntan cream and a coaster rested on the table. She carefully placed her martini glass on the coaster.

"Make yourself comfortable, Mr. Haskell." Then she turned away every so slightly and dropped her top. She took her sweet time meticulously folding the tiny thing before placing it on the table next to her drink, once folded it looked smaller than the coaster. She laid down on the lawn chair, stretched out, facedown ready to bake in the relentless sun.

"Say." She turned her head in my direction. "Be a dear and make yourself useful, will you? Put that suntan cream on my back." She pointed to the tube next to her folded top.

Oddly, given the circumstances, my first thought was about her dogs. If she was setting me up, and they so much as appeared, I planned to shoot the damn things without a second thought. I squirted a puddle of cream into my hand, and then nervously looked around for the dogs to appear.

"What are you worried about? I told you before. It's very private back here. No one can see us. We could do absolutely anything, and no one would ever know." She rolled onto her side, exposing a very impressive chest without even the hint of a tan line. She reached for her martini glass and took a long, slow sip. She held her position and smiled.

"Real nice and private back here, isn't it?" She took another sip and licked her lips. Her eyes never left mine.

I could tell she was waiting for me to act stupid, babble some dumb guy line, or look away and comment on the flowers in the garden.

"Lola, you got a hell of a great rack."

"Enhanced," she bragged.

"Real nice. Now roll over, will you? So I can do your back and get this suntan glop off my hands."

"Oh, for a moment I wasn't sure what that was." She giggled, took another long sip, shrugged, and set her glass back on the coaster before settling in, face down.

I began applying the cream. I purposely missed an area about the size of a silver dollar on her back, just where I thought the hooks from her bra would rub. I figured forty minutes in this sun without protection would leave a nice burn. I worked my way down to her hips.

"Do my buns too, will you? It feels so good."

I squirted the suntan cream directly onto her rear.

"Whoa, that's cold."

"Oh, sorry." I wasn't in the least.

"Better rub it in deep."

I massaged the suntan cream. I'll give her this much…she was toned. No doubt about it. She arched her back, raising her rear suggestively. I got up and grabbed a nearby chair.

"Afraid I'm too much?" she asked, face still buried in the pillow.

"Afraid? No, just on kind of a short time frame and I never like to rush."

"Really?" she said into the pillow sounding genuinely curious.

"Lola, remember you told me about a guy who used to work for you, Bernie Sneen?"

"Oh, yes, I do. As a matter of fact, we had a call from the police about him. Involved in some dreadful accident, I guess. They wanted some background information. Not that we could tell them much, other than he was caught stealing."

"Did you tell them anything else?"

"Anything else? No, there was nothing to tell. I suppose I could have mentioned you thought he was the one who ran into us. Attempted to kill us with his car, but that's really conjecture now, isn't it? I didn't want to get you in trouble. Besides, what difference would it make? He wandered around barefoot and then

106

taped himself to the train tracks. Sad really. Not to speak ill of the dead or anything, but I would guess he quite possibly never, ever, accomplished anything positive in his whole miserable little life."

"I guess that pretty much sums it up."

"Maybe. It's just all sort of sad, you know? There are so many wonderful things to do and try in this world. Some are just there for the taking." She said then turned her head and squinted at me.

"Yeah, right. Hey, did you guys get my invoice? I could save you the cost of a stamp if you…"

"I think he put something in the mail to you the other day."

"Mr. Swirlee?"

"Yes."

"Okay, thanks. Look, I better get going. Mind letting me out the front?"

"Tell you what…just go out the back gate. The lock release is right inside the garage door. Push the button and it's good for ten seconds. Mind getting me another refill before you go?" she said, then held her glass out, wiggling it back and forth at me while licking her lips.

I stood up, picked her top off the table and used it to wipe the excess suntan cream off my hands.

"As a matter of fact, I do mind," I said, then strode toward the back gate.

Chapter Twenty-Six

I was still parked in front of Mr. Swirlee's when I phoned Detective Manning and left a message. I glanced in the rearview mirror after I hung up and watched as a large black Mercedes turned onto the side street. It was followed by a white Escalade. Through the tinted windows I could just make out two large silhouettes in the front seat of the Escalade.

I pulled away from the curb, rounded the next corner, then slowed opposite the alley and watched just as Mr. Swirlee drove into his garage. The Escalade pulled in front of the garage, and my two pals from the other night casually climbed out.

They actually looked larger in the daylight, even from this distance. They glanced in my direction, but gave no indication they recognized me before they strolled into the back yard where Lola was presumably still stretched out.

Another one of those coincidences I didn't like. Christ, I was beginning to sound like Detective Manning.

I drove home and sorted through the mail. There were three grocery circulars, an overdraft notice from my bank and the letter from Mr. Swirlee. I opened the envelope expecting to see a check. What I got was the invoice I had sent, with a note scrawled across the front in red ink.

"Please furnish signed documentation of our contractual agreement."

Documentation! They'd signed my contract less than twenty-four hours before I mailed my invoice. I phoned Mr. Swirlee, left a message, reminding him they'd signed my contract on his kitchen counter. I finished with a line indicating I planned to deliver my invoice, expecting payment in full, and to please call me if he had any questions or concerns. I hoped I sounded suitably upset.

I drifted down to The Spot, fortified myself with a few beers, then phoned Jill. It had never served me well to drink and dial.

"Oh hi, Dev. Look I..." She sounded cheery enough.

"I thought I'd just check in, see how your head was after last night," I interrupted.

"My head? Fine, why?"

"Well, you know, I feel kind of bad, having to run off last night. I had my meeting this morning..."

"Who's that?" A male voice in the background on her end came across the line.

"Oh yeah, your morning meeting. I'd like to hear about it but, well, I'm sort of busy right now. Look, I hate to rush off, but..."

"Who is that?" The same male voice asked, but this time a bit more forcefully.

"Sorry, guess I caught you at a bad time. Hope I didn't cause you any problems. I'll talk to you later," I said, then hung up. Serves her right, I thought.

I phoned the sometimes available Heidi Bauer, a friend with benefits, but had to leave a message. I hoped I didn't sound too drunk or too desperate. I tried a couple of other numbers from the past. It seemed everyone was busy at the moment, or was it just the goddamn Caller I.D.?

About a half hour later my phone rang. Unfortunately not a date, but Detective Manning. This time I thought thank God for Caller I.D. and let his call drop into my message center.

Chapter Twenty-Seven

The phone woke me about 9:45 the following morning. By the time I found it under the couch it was in the message mode. I climbed off the couch, made coffee, used the bathroom, then checked my messages. There were actually three.

The first was from Patti, a gorgeous Asian American woman I used to date. The last time she spoke to me she told me, in no uncertain terms, to never, ever to contact her again.

Emboldened by beer and just plain desperate, I had a foggy recollection of phoning her last night sometime after midnight. Her message was about the same as the last time she spoke to me. Except a little more forceful and a lot more profane.

The second message was from Jill.

"Hi, this is Jill. Sorry I was unable to talk when you called earlier. Please give me a call when it's convenient. Thanks."

The third message was from Detective Manning.

"Haskell. Manning. Returning your call."

Charming.

I decided to take the best of the three and phoned Jill.

"Hi Jill, Dev Haskell."

"Oh, hey, thanks for returning my call. Maybe I should ask you. How's the head?"

I cleared my throat a bit. "What do you mean?"

"You just sounded like you weren't feeling any pain last night when you phoned."

"Oh sorry, no. Actually I was doing some computer stuff and was just a little preoccupied is all."

"You always slur your words when you work on your computer?"

"Hey, Jill, I hope I didn't goof up your night or anything. I didn't realize you were with someone. I'm sorry if my call…"

"With someone? Oh god, you idiot. I was visiting my grandfather. He's in assisted living now. He sort of wanders, you know. So when he's having a good spell I want to make the best of it. Otherwise, I would have loved to get together."

"How about sometime today?" I asked.

"Tonight would work better. I've gotta meet with the insurance people again, a couple of contractors. Free for dinner?"

"Yeah, but only if I buy. You know Shamrock's?"

"Yeah," she scoffed, like it was a stupid question. "Seven?"

"I'm there. Look, I gotta run. I can see a contractor pulling up in front right now. See you tonight," she said and hung up.

I phoned Manning. Amazingly he answered.

"Yeah."

"Detective Manning, Dev Haskell."

"I can see that."

"Any progress on Bernie Sneen?"

"I really don't care to comment about an ongoing investigation."

112

"I might have something for you."

"Such as?"

"You interested in trading a little information?"

"Are you interested in being held without bail?"

"You aren't going to do that, and we both know it. Look, just tell me…you mentioned a dog bite on Bernie Sneen. Was it a big dog, a Chihuahua, what?"

"We don't know the breed, but I can tell you this much…it was big and damn vicious, tore a chuck of meat right out of your buddy's ass. Your turn."

"I went to see my former clients yesterday…"

"And their name is?"

"Mr. Swirlee. Actually, I spoke with…what did you call her, Loretta?"

"The girlfriend? Lucille."

"Yeah, I know her as Lola. Anyway, talking with her yesterday, she mentioned Bernie getting hit by the train, then mentioned the duct tape. She said he taped himself to the train tracks after walking around barefoot. You'd told me you were keeping that quiet. Maybe you mentioned it to her, maybe not, so I just thought you should be aware."

"How did she phrase it, exactly?"

"Exactly? She said he never ever accomplished anything in his life. He wandered around barefoot and then taped himself to the train tracks, is what she said. Or at least that's how I remember it."

"You react when she said that?"

"No, there were a couple of things going on at the time and…"

"Such as?"

"Not getting paid for starters. I sent that bastard an invoice. They wanted documentation. It's all bullshit. They're stalling."

"You talking a lot of money?"

"Not really, certainly not to them. But it's more the principle with me, you know?"

"Yeah, you're a principled kind of guy. Anything else?" he asked.

"No, just thought you should know. Hope it helps."

"Thanks, always nice to hear from a concerned citizen."

"Yeah, well, let me know if..." but he'd already hung up.

Chapter Twenty-Eight

Jill appeared through the side door of Shamrock's twenty minutes late in white linen slacks and a beige blouse. She looked worth the wait.

"Hey, sorry I'm late. I had to give Annie a lift," she said, giving me a kiss on the cheek.

"Everything okay?"

"Yeah, just pain-in-the-butt stuff. Brakes went out, and she had to get there before seven to pick her car up. Her boyfriend had to work late, so she called me, last minute."

"Sauvignon Blanc," she said to the waitress, a frizzy red-headed girl, who had just barely stepped up to our table.

"Another beer, Sir?"

"Please." I returned my attention to Jill. "Hey, I spoke to that Jennifer here the other night, but I haven't seen her yet. I wonder if she's working?" I was absently looking around.

"Did you ask anyone?"

"Ask? No, not yet. I was just looking…"

"Typical," she smiled.

Her wine and my next beer arrived a few minutes later.

"Can you tell me, is Jennifer working tonight?" Jill asked the waitress.

"What was her last name, again?"

"McCauley, Jennifer McCauley," I said.

"Oh, didn't you guys hear? She was in a car accident."

"A car accident? No, we didn't hear anything. Least I didn't. You?" Jill turned to look at me.

I shook my head.

"What happened? Is she okay?"

"Well, she's in the hospital. She'll be okay, I guess, but she was pretty banged up. Some guy hit her from behind and just kept on pushing her. She was driving home last night. I think she was on the High Bridge at the time. She's lucky he didn't push her off or something, you know?"

"Did they get the guy?" I asked. I was pretty sure I knew the answer.

"No, it was after her shift, so sorta late at night, you know? Hit and run. I guess all she saw were these big headlights. You know the real bright kind. Her car was totaled. She's lucky she wasn't killed is all I can say. Anyway, you guys ready to order?"

"Maybe give us a minute," I said.

"God, the poor girl," Jill said after taking a big sip of wine. "Sometimes people are just crazy." She grabbed a menu and opened it.

"Jill, is it just me or does it seem a little strange that after your fire, the only potential witness is rear ended on the High Bridge by a big car with bright lights?"

"What?"

"Jennifer's accident. Mr. Swirlee gets broadsided in a hit-and-run. Your fire. Now this Jennifer in a hit-and-run. What does all this tell you?"

116

"You're some kind of a paranoid freak?" She didn't even look up from her menu.

"What about the brakes on your sister's car?"

"Hey look. Annie doesn't think to put oil into her car until the light comes on. As for her brakes, they've been making noise for five weeks. Her solution is to just turn up the radio. God knows she didn't pay attention to me bitching about it. What are you going to have?"

"Another beer."

Chapter Twenty-Nine

The following morning, armed with the remnants of a hangover and the not-so-pleasant memory of Mr. Swirlee's note scrawled across my invoice, I decided to pay him a call.

He answered the phone at the gate and buzzed me in himself. The dogs were nowhere to be seen. Although I'd just spoken to him less than a minute before I had to ring the doorbell and wait. I rang it again.

After I rang the third time the door opened almost immediately. Mr. Swirlee stood there with a chrome metal cane. Most of his weight rested on his right leg. His right hand held onto the large brass door knob and his left arm rested against the door frame, blocking my way. His injured leg was set inside a grey plastic walking cast and held in place with a series of black nylon straps. He wore pressed, loose-fitting navy blue trousers, an expensive looking polo shirt and a dark scowl.

"What the hell is it?" he snapped.

"Well, for starters it's my invoice. You sent it back to me."

I pulled the envelope out of my back pocket, took the invoice out and unfolded it. I hoped his note, foolishly scrawled in red across the bottom would be self-explanatory and he would just cut me a check.

"So?"

I waited a beat then said,

"But you signed a contract with me less than twenty-four hours beforehand."

"I did?"

"Yeah, we were right in the kitchen, don't you remember? You forced a can of Busch light on me."

"Perhaps, if you could show me the contract, I would be able to remember."

'You pompous prick. You know damn well you signed it. You're just trying to rip me off,' I thought. Then I said, "I'd be happy to, Sir. I have it right here." I pulled the contract out of my back pocket, unfolded it, handed it to him and stood there looking quite satisfied.

"This isn't my signature," he said, squinting at the pinkish mess that was Lola's beer soaked signature. He stabbed the contract back toward me like that settled the matter.

"Well, no, I mean that's Lola's signature, your wife, but you were there when she signed it. In fact you even said she takes care of those details for you."

"She has no legal status. Wife? Hardly. I think you fucked up, pal. Good-bye." He attempted to close the door.

I wedged my left foot against the door to stop him from slamming it closed.

"Now just hang on there, damn it. Mr. Swirlee, Sir. If you think I'm..."

He slammed his chrome cane down hard on the bridge of my left foot.

"Arghhh," I screamed, but it was cut off the moment he jammed the cane, two-handed, up between my legs. I doubled over, grabbed my crotch, and sank to my knees. Swirlee spun his cane like some high school majorette and clubbed me over the head, full force, as if he was splitting firewood. I saw stars and collapsed onto his welcome mat.

"I'm gonna let the damn dogs loose. You'd better get your ass out of here, ya bum!" He turned and hobbled as fast as his cane allowed down the hallway toward the rear of the house.

I lay in the doorway, vaguely aware I was bleeding from my head wound. I gasped a few times and took some deep breaths. I used the door frame for support as I slowly struggled to my feet and swallowed my stomach back down. At the far end of the hallway Swirlee glanced over his shoulder, then hobbled into the darkened dining room. I heard barking. I reached inside the entryway and pushed the button for the lock release at the front gate, slammed the door shut behind me and made my way toward the safety of the street as best I could. I was halfway to the gate when I heard the dogs barking and scratching viciously on the inside of the front door.

From somewhere deep in my memory I heard Detective Manning's voice say, '*I can tell you this much...it was big and damn vicious, tore a chunk of meat right out of your buddy's ass.*'

I made it to the gate, pulled it open, and slammed it closed behind me just as the front door flew open and Mr. Swirlee released his dogs. They shot out the door, ears back, barking and growling, full speed to the gate. In little more than a second or two they'd pulled up with their snouts thrust through the wrought iron fence, snarling and yelping at me as I hobbled across the sidewalk to my car.

"Are you okay?" someone asked out there on the periphery of my senses.

I was dazed and just wanted the safety of my Lincoln.

A woman's voice asked, "Excuse me, Sir, you're bleeding. Did you fall? Are you all right?"

Some guy said,

"Better stay back, Marjorie. I'm calling 911."

I turned to look at them, had the vague sense they were standing still, but everything else was spinning.

"Yes, I'd like to report some sort of burglar-type person. He's bleeding and seems to be on drugs or something. He's just…"

The male voice faded away as I climbed into my car and drove off. There was the sharp screech of tires from somewhere behind me, rubber on pavement, followed immediately by a very long blast from an angry car horn.

<u>Chapter Thirty</u>

It was the pounding on my door that eventually woke me.

"Are you all right, Sir?" the officer asked.

I lowered the car window.

"Yeah, just closing my eyes for a moment." I was parked in my driveway although I couldn't remember how I got there.

The officer was polite, looked to be about fifteen, and then asked one of those cop questions that really wasn't a question.

"Would you mind turning off your vehicle and stepping outside, Sir?"

I did as instructed.

"Do you have any identification?"

I handed him my wallet. Then, I noticed for the first time another officer on the far side of the Lincoln. A second squad car had just pulled up and effectively blocked the driveway. I felt faint and leaned back against the Lincoln.

"Have you been drinking, Sir?"

"No."

"Would you mind taking your license out of your wallet?"

I took the license out, and handed it to him.

"So, Mr. Haskell," he said, then proceeded to ask a few more questions that might best be summed up as, "What the hell is going on?"

I submitted to a breathalyzer test in the back of the squad car and then was carted down to the police station for booking. I was charged with trespassing, attempted burglary and assault.

It was close to ten that night when I phoned Heidi and asked her to come down and bail me out.

"What did you do this time?" she asked after hearing me explain.

"I just told you, nothing. Look, can you just come and get me out? Please?"

"I'm busy right now," she half whispered.

"Oh, God, you're involved in some damned orgy or something, aren't you?"

"Well, that makes it easy. I'll see you in the morning, bye."

"No, wait, wait, Heidi don't..." I mumbled, but she'd already hung up her phone.

"That didn't seem to go your way." The desk sergeant chuckled. "Not to worry, you can call her again in the morning. Come on, time for sweet dreams," he said as he led me back to my cell.

Heidi bailed me out about eleven the following morning. We were in her car before she said anything other than hello. I had the sense she wasn't in the best of moods.

"What the hell did you do?" She was looking at my forehead as she cranked the key in her ignition.

I opened my mouth to speak.

"No, don't say a word. You're just damn lucky I'm even here. Please spare me whatever tale you have. I don't want to hear it. By the way, you look like shit.

You look like you got run over by a truck, and what's with Mount Everest there on your forehead? Oh, and while we're on the subject, a shower wouldn't do you any harm, man," she said, then lowered her window and drove off.

Despite the lecture, she was a good friend, and unfortunately this was not the first time she'd bailed me out.

"All I'm going to say is that what has been done to me is one great, big, giant mistake. That's all."

She glared over at me. "Done to you? Who do you think you're kidding? Hey, Butthead, Jesus, I just posted bail for you because one of your clients, Mr. Swirlee, filed assault charges against you. Seems now you're pissing off the elite in town."

"I told you it's not my fault."

"Oh please, you are forbidden to say one damn word."

She was a redhead this week, auburn actually. It looked kind of nice and was decidedly better than some of the things she had done in the past with her hair. She'd gone through a sort of punk-rocker red, blue, pink phase that was really tough to take on an over thirty-five, fairly wealthy, financial trader.

"I can't believe they're jacking me around like this over a couple of bucks."

"I thought you weren't going to say anything," she snapped.

"Okay, okay, I'm through. I promise. So did you have a nice night?" I asked then turned to stare out the car window.

She ignored my question for a block or two before she launched into her next lecture.

"This is getting old. I'm sick and tired of always being your first call for help every time you screw up."

We'd just passed the Xcel center, heading up the hill toward the Cathedral. I felt resigned to my fate.

"Yeah."

"No, not yeah. What is this? Three, four times I've had to post bail?"

"I already told you this isn't my fault."

"It never is, is it? It must be my fault then. It's my fault for not having anything better to do than take your idiot phone call. First call for help...apparently that's all I'm good for."

"Hey, they're screwing me on my invoice. They tried to run a young gal off the high bridge. They tied Bernie to the railroad tracks and let a train run over him. They fire-bombed the ice cream place. And dipshit Swirlee tried to beat me to death yesterday afternoon before he attempted to feed me to his dogs."

She looked over at me wide eyed.

"Are you nuts? Did you go to the cops?"

"Where did we just come from?"

"Who's doing all this?"

"Mr. Swirlee. He's..."

"He's your client, for God's sake. Now he's trying to kill you?"

"Yeah, haven't you been listening?"

"I don't want to hear anymore. You are delusional. Get out," she said, screeching to a stop in front of my place.

My car was still sitting in the driveway. I looked over at her and asked, "You want to come in for a drink?"

"Get the hell out of my car!" she screamed. She waited just a fraction of a second after I got out then sped off.

Chapter Thirty-One

I took some painkillers I found in the medicine cabinet and went to bed. It felt good to sleep in my bed as opposed to on the couch or in a cell. I rolled out of bed close to noon the following morning. I gulped down four Tylenol Extra Strength and stared at myself in the mirror.

It looked like a mountain range had erupted across the top of my forehead where Swirlee clubbed me with his cane. It was raw, tender to the touch, and throbbed. I had one hell of a headache and not so much as a drop of alcohol consumption to blame for it.

I was drinking coffee while holding an ice pack gingerly against my head when the phone rang.

"Hello."

"I see you've been a busy boy." It was Manning, obviously taking some degree of enjoyment from my plight.

"What are you talking about?" I asked, hoping it might be something else.

"Don't play cute, Haskell. I've seen the list of charges your so-called client filed against you. Half the force has already volunteered to bring you in."

"It's all a bunch of bullshit. I didn't do anything except suggest my invoice should be paid."

"So you say." He laughed.

I thought I might have said too much already. After a long pause Manning said,

"You should fit in real well with all your pals already serving in Stillwater. I'll enjoy visiting."

"Other than harassment, was there a purpose to this call?"

"Not really, except I just wanted to let you know we're all thinking of you. Bye."

Bad news traveled fast.

I phoned Heidi and groveled my thanks as I left a message. Then I sat over another cup of coffee, a fresh ice pack and came to the conclusion I was going after Mr. Swirlee. If anyone was going to be serving time, it was him. I showered, dressed, and decided to go talk to Jennifer McCauley in the hospital.

It was approaching one in the afternoon. Another hot, muggy, cloudless day. I'd have killed for this weather come winter, but right now snow and minus ten was sounding pretty good.

I tried to pull a baseball cap over my head wound, but the bump was too large and painful. So I went bareheaded.

My car sat in the driveway, all closed up and baking in the relentless sun. It was about one hundred and thirty in there when I opened the door. Since my air conditioner was broken I had to wait for a minute or two while the interior cooled down. Eventually, I backed out of the driveway, already drowning in sweat. The shocks on the Lincoln creaked as I bounced into the street. There was something slightly unpleasant in the air. It just hung there with the

127

humidity. I guessed the restaurant across the street had some garbage rotting in a dumpster.

Chapter Thirty-Two

Jennifer McCauley was sharing a hospital room with a little girl I guessed to be about ten. Her name was La Tasha. She was in the far bed next to the window and had a leg in a cast suspended in traction. She wore large red-framed glasses and was hidden behind a thick Harry Potter book. As she read she moved her lips. The room was overflowing with flowers and stuffed animals, all of which seemed to be addressed to Jennifer.

Jennifer looked awfully black and blue. She sported a number of scrapes and cuts on her arms and face, both eyes were black, and her nose had obviously been broken. But she wasn't hooked up to any monitors. She had one IV in the back of her left hand, and a bag of clear solution hung on a wheeled stand next to the bed. She was sitting up in bed, eating a pink yogurt, and watching a soap opera.

"Hi, Jennifer, how are you doing?" I was standing in the doorway.

"Oh wow, Declan," she said.

"Devlin, but call me Dev, please. Hey, I was down at Shamrock's and heard your news. You okay?"

"No, I'm bored silly. Supposed to get out of here this afternoon. My mom will be down about three. I'm gonna stay at my folks' for a while, till I get back to normal. Whatever that is," she joked.

"Probably a good idea."

"You're not looking so hot." She inclined her head a fraction of an inch to indicate the throbbing knot on my forehead.

"Yeah, comes with the business."

"Man, what? Arresting some major criminal? Beating up some gangsters?" She sounded deadly serious.

I didn't have the heart to tell her some half-crippled geriatric blind-sided me and then kicked the shit out of me on his doorstep. So, I borrowed a line from Manning.

"Yeah, it's still an ongoing investigation. I can't really comment."

"Cool." Then she grinned from ear to ear.

"Tell me about your deal, what happened?"

"Oh, my, God! It was so scary. I finished my shift, had a couple of drinks with Jeff and Tommy. I think Georgie was there, too. Anyway, I drove home, it's like maybe one-fifteen, one-thirty. I'm not blotto or anything. I'm going over the High Bridge. No cars around. No one coming toward me, no one behind me. I get about halfway across the bridge, I see some headlights in my rearview mirror. And they're like getting closer, really fast. I'm thinking, oh, my, God, that asshole is really speeding and then the next thing I know he's coming up right behind me."

"Did he honk, or flash his lights or anything?"

Her hair was still curly and bounced back and forth as she shook her head no.

"Nothing, he just raced across the bridge and plowed into me. He must have been really drunk, you know? Didn't stop or nothing. It was like he was aiming at me."

"What kind of a car do you drive?"

"Totaled, as of now. Cops said I'm lucky to be alive."

"What kind of car did you drive?"

"Blue."

"Do you know what make?"

"A Camry."

"A Toyota."

"I think so."

"Did you get a look at the car that hit you?"

She shook her head again.

"No, I saw the headlights, realized he was really going fast, and then boom. He just slammed right into me. He kept pushing like I was just in the way or something, the asshole. Oops, sorry La Tasha, that just slipped out."

La Tasha looked up from her book for half a moment, grinned then returned to her page.

"Anyway, he sort of spun the whole car around, pushed me over the curb, and against the guardrail. I guess I was unconscious. I sort of don't remember that part."

"Maybe that's a good thing," I said.

She shrugged, nodded, took another spoonful of pink yogurt and glanced up at her soap opera.

"No idea what the car looked like?"

"No, sorry."

"Any boyfriend problems or arguments with someone? Anything that might cause somebody to go after you?"

"No, nothing. The police asked me the same thing. I really can't think of anything. I date a couple of different guys, nothing serious. Play on the softball team. We're really bad, but we have fun."

"Anyone who might think you're stealing a boyfriend or tips?"

"Nope, nothing like that. Actually, I'm pretty boring. Hey, are you thinking of taking my case? That would really be cool."

"I tell you what I'll keep an ear to the ground, see if something turns up. But no promises, okay?"

"Yeah, I guess, except if you find whoever it was, it's okay with me if you shoot them." She didn't smile, or blink.

"I'll keep that in mind, Jennifer. You rest up, get better…here." I handed her another one of my cards. "Anything turns up, you call me. Promise?"

"Yeah, I promise." She smiled.

Chapter Thirty-Three

I phoned Jill after chatting with Jennifer. She answered just as I stepped out of the air-conditioned hospital and into a wall of blistering heat and humidity. The hot sun felt like someone held a magnifying glass over the wound on my forehead.

"Guess who I just talked to?" I asked.

"A bartender?"

"Not a bad idea, but sadly, no. Jennifer McCauley."

"Where'd you run into her?"

"I didn't run into her, I went to visit her in the hospital. I'm just leaving now. She's hoping to get out later today."

"How is she?"

"How is she? Lucky to be alive, I'd say. She's cut, scraped, black and blue all over, but nothing that won't heal. Bottom line is she's a very lucky young woman."

"You still feeling paranoid?"

"I don't know that I ever was. But I don't think this was some random hit-and-run, if that's what you mean. The way she described it to me, someone set out to nail her, and damn near succeeded. If it wasn't for that railing on the High Bridge, her car would have dropped a hundred and sixty feet to the river below."

"I don't know. It all seems a little far-fetched to me, I…"

"Far-fetched? Didn't someone fire-bomb your business?"

"Yeah, I know, but I'm only suggesting that to tie her accident into our fire still seems to be a stretch."

"Well, I'll keep my assumptions in the maybe range, but a strong maybe. Look, I'm at my car, so I better go. I'll call you if something develops."

"I'm not holding my breath. Bye," she said and hung up.

I had parked on the street since I didn't have five bucks for the ramp. The Lincoln shimmered and baked in the afternoon heat. Even though I'd left the windows down it still felt like an oven inside. Some bird had crapped on the inside of the backseat. That same rotted-something odor was in the air and I wondered if maybe it wasn't coming from the river. I opened the doors to try and get something like a breeze going through. That didn't work, so I finally drove away, hoping to get some air circulating.

I headed down to the police impound lot, the one on Barge Channel Road. As one might expect by the street name, it was close to the Mississippi River. The smell hanging in the air seemed even stronger down here, and I was convinced it had to be something in the river. Whatever it was, it was getting close to nauseating.

For a city that spent a lot of time and effort over the years attempting to be more consumer friendly, the St. Paul Impound Lot had somehow missed the boat. Then again if you were down here to begin with you weren't going to have a positive experience, so why

134

bother? The entry path wove a fifty-yard zigzag pattern toward the front door. The path was enclosed along both sides with ten-foot-high Cyclone fencing topped off with rolls of concertina wire. Razor wire was strung back and forth over the path. It gave one pause, wondering who would ever want to break into the office to begin with.

I entered through the worn, graffiti covered, industrial grey door and then climbed the grimy steps up to the lobby. More graffiti-covered grimy walls and a groaning noise oozing from an inefficient window air conditioner that pumped heat into the tiny lobby. The office was really nothing more than a government issue desk sitting behind six layers of finger-printed, bullet-proof glass.

A couple stood stooped over, arguing through a metal vent with the bland-faced civil servant on the far side of the grimy glass. They weren't getting very far. They smelled of cigarette smoke and liquor. After about five minutes of restating their case multiple times they slid a debit card into the depression on the well- worn counter. The clerk took his sweet time, examined both sides of the card, carefully entered the payment amount on some sort of device and then waited, and waited. After an hour or two he painstakingly tore the perforated edges off their receipt. He carefully aligned the corners and folded the receipt, then ran a finger slowly along the fold to create the perfect crease. He cautiously slid the receipt out to them and flashed just the slightest hint of a smile.

"What an asshole," the woman said under her breath as she marched back down the stairs.

I stepped into the space they had recently occupied. Just a hint of cigarette and alcohol lingered in the air. I stared through the glass at the clerk. His name tag read Loren.

I'd first met Loren Baker while bailing out a car about eighteen years ago. I bought him a beer a few nights later when he'd already had too many. He seemed just as dull now as he did back then. His nickname was "Forlorn", not that he had many friends who used his nickname. For some reason he seemed to like me, and I'd always felt it could be helpful to have some pull at the impound lot.

"Hey there, Dev, how's it going? Don't tell me they dragged another one of your horseshit cars in here?"

"Amazingly, no, they didn't. Nice to see you, Loren. How's life treating you?" I tried to sound sincere.

"Things are going good, Dev. Thanks for asking. We should get together sometime. Been awhile," he said.

"Yeah, it has." I was thinking eighteen years wasn't long enough.

"We could chase some tail," he said, sounding hopeful.

Not a chance in hell.

"That would be fun." I smiled.

"So what do you need?"

"Actually, Loren, I just wanted to look at a vehicle, or what's left of it. Get a sense of the damage done. This was a hit-and-run from about three nights back over on the High Bridge. From what I hear there might not be much to look at."

"Name on the title?" he asked, unwilling to engage in any further small talk.

"McCauley, Jennifer"

"That with one or two Ls?" he asked, bending over a laptop. As he typed, the white/blue screen reflected off the coke bottle lenses on his glasses.

"Just one," I said, then spelled Jennifer's last name for him, and got a nod in return. He turned round, pulled a sheet of paper off a printer, and pushed it out through the window well.

"It's in slot thirty-seven. Just junk, not sure why we got it. 'Less they're holding it for some ongoing investigation. Course, then it should be over at BCA. Anyone killed?"

"No, amazingly."

"That's why, then. Out the door, show that receipt to Jerry. Have him point you in the right direction."

I thanked 'Forlorn' then thanked God I didn't work in this miserable place and went out to the lot.

Jerry weighed in at about four hundred pounds and looked like he hadn't gotten up from behind his desk in the past twenty years. He made no effort to do so when I handed him the receipt. He looked up from his paperback, a romance, and he sighed, "Out the door, first left, three rows back, then left again. Metal tag IDs the slot. Not much left of that one," he added, and then returned to his romance.

There was a part of me that wanted to ask him when the last time was he had a date? Touched his toes? Hell, even saw his toes? Instead, I smiled and said, "Thank you for your help," and walked back out into the oppressive heat.

Jennifer, "Forlorn", and Jerry weren't kidding. There wasn't much left. Jennifer McCauley was a very lucky young lady and damn lucky to even be alive, let alone not in critical condition. Her Camry had been assaulted from all angles, rammed and pounded into about a third of its original size. The damaged areas all had one thing in common, streaks and chips of a sort of cream-colored paint.

I reached in my back pocket and took out the envelope from Mr. Swirlee, the one he had used to return my invoice. Using a thumbnail, I managed to scrape some decent sized paint chips off the Camry and get them into the envelope. I had a sneaking suspicion the chips would match a certain Escalade. I decided to pay another visit to Mr. Swirlee.

Chapter Thirty-Four

The smell was even stronger when I got back to my car. It just sort of hung in the air. I couldn't understand how anyone could work down in this area. You'd never get the smell out of your clothes.

Based on the throbbing from my forehead, not to mention the assault charges I was facing, I had second thoughts and figured it might make sense to stay away from Mr. Swirlee for the moment. Instead, I drove out I-94 to a Cadillac dealership for some in-depth evidence analysis.

The dealership sat in the middle of four acres of gleaming automobiles. It was a one-story glass and white enamel building with large signs running the length of the windows proclaiming "Immediate Financing available!" I parked the Lincoln next to the entry and walked in.

I wasn't more than three steps in the door when an elegant, blonde sales rep appeared out of nowhere and swooped down.

"Hi, help you?" She was gorgeous and stared at my forehead, probably wondering if I was growing a second head.

Despite their signs there was no way in hell I would ever qualify for financing, immediate or otherwise. Still, I guessed it wouldn't hurt matters to toss some of my personal charm her way.

"Just wanted to take a look around," I said.

She blinked her gorgeous green eyes away from my forehead.

"What did you have in mind?"

Like every other idiot I thought *nothing on the showroom floor*. She wore a small gold cross around her neck. Christ hanging there all day, just staring into her cleavage...lucky guy. I caught the subtle scent of her perfume, a pleasant change from the rotten river I'd been sniffing fifteen minutes earlier.

"Sir?"

"Oh, sorry. I was just remembering a meeting I've got, but maybe, if you had a minute or two, you could show me around." I glanced down at the cross for another brief moment.

She must have been a fairly experienced salesperson. She smiled seductively, sized me up as a complete waste of time, then pointed around the showroom and said, "Tell you what...all of our models are out on the floor here. Stickers on the windows will tell you the price. Feel free to look around and then let me know if you have any specific questions." With that she turned on her heel and walked back to a small office, probably thinking she'd have better luck calling random people out of the phone book than wasting time talking to me.

I strolled around for three minutes, trying to pretend I was a qualified buyer. Some sweaty guy who I guessed was from the repair shop strolled in the front door. He wore a uniform of blue pants and a blue shirt. The shirt had a white name tag that read Gary in red letters sewn just above the pocket. He had his nose wrinkled and sort of shuddered to himself as he walked back to what was the lounge area. It was decorated with brown vinyl couches, dog-eared magazines, and the scent of coffee that had been on the burner for about six hours too long.

"Jesus, you get a whiff of outside? Smells like a fart contest, man alive."

I knew what he was talking about. I'd been smelling it all day long. Whatever was in the air, it had carried all the way out here to suburbia. I grabbed a brochure on the Escalade line, complete with color options and walked out. He was right. That same rotted smell just seemed to hang in the heavy air.

I drove home, tossed down a couple more Tylenol and then sat at my dining-room table prepared to do careful scientific analysis while I sipped a Leinenkugel. I opened the Escalade brochure, took the paint chips I scraped off Jennifer's wreck, and laid them on the brochure color chart. I came up with an exact color match, white diamond tri-coat. Mr. Swirlee and his thugs.

Chapter Thirty-Five

I was about to get another beer when the phone rang.

"Haskell Investigations."

"Hi Dev, Jill. Just checking to see how you're doing. How's the head?"

"It'll be okay," I said, not adding, "after this beer."

"Look, I'm running around, but I was thinking maybe I could bring you over some dinner, if I wasn't imposing or anything."

"Oh, you don't have to do that." I managed to add just a hint of desperation in my tone to suggest it would be a very good idea.

"Yeah, I know I don't have to, but if I wasn't imposing, I'd like to. Unless you've got other plans."

"No, no other plans. I would like that. What time were you thinking?"

"Six okay?"

"Six works for me. See you then."

I had ice cream and gin in the freezer, cranberry juice and beer in the fridge. Other than clean sheets and hiding the stack of unpaid bills and final-notice warnings I was all set.

Jill arrived at six on the dot.

I opened the front door, she gave me a kiss on the cheek and by way of greeting she said, "God, it smells awful around here."

"It's been like that all day. You get it over by you? I think it's coming off the river, with all the heat and everything."

"No, it's really stinky, though. How's that forehead?" she asked as she brushed past.

I was expecting a pizza and maybe a six-pack. Instead she carried two grocery bags with a lot of little white containers and two bottles of chilled wine. I remembered her mind set the last time she drank two bottles of wine. Things were looking up.

"I hope you like Thai food. There's a great takeout over on University," she said, walking into my kitchen.

"I love it." I was unaware of ever eating any before.

"What is that thing?" she asked looking at my stuffed Muskie hanging on the kitchen wall.

"I caught that a couple of years back," I said.

"A Muskie, right?"

"Yeah." I was surprised she knew.

"Barely large enough to keep…fact it might be undersized, barely legal. You must not do a lot of fishing. At least not a lot of Muskie fishing."

"Hey, how about a Cosmo, just to get you started?" I asked, quickly changing the subject then cautioned myself about over-serving.

"I better just stick with the wine, if it's all the same. Thanks," she said, taking a final look at my Muskie, shaking her head, and then getting to work on our meal.

Over dinner I showed her the paint chips and the Escalade brochure, then explained how I thought it had been Mr. Swirlee's goons who rammed Jennifer

McCauley on the High Bridge. Then I told her about Bernie Sneen, the night I tried to place a bet at the ice cream truck and the cream-colored Escalade with the two thugs.

"I'm starting to believe you, Dev. So, just for the sake of discussion, let's say you're right. The question still remains, why? I can't for the life of me think that we offered any competition to him. But, let's say in some warped way we did. We certainly don't anymore, not since the fire. So why ram that Jennifer girl's car? And why tape some guy to the train tracks? That's just bizarre." Then she held out her glass and I drained the remainder of the first bottle into it.

"It's not the ice cream. It's the operation, Mr. Swirlee, his gambling operation."

She took a sip of wine, then swirled her finger in the peanut sauce and licked it off her finger, seductively.

"Okay. I'm still back to the same question. What does that have to do with anything we know about? It just doesn't make sense. That's all I'm saying."

I couldn't disagree. I had all sorts of random ideas, but they all seemed to get more and more disconnected the closer I got to Mr. Swirlee. He was the key, Swirlee. It had to be.

Some time later, after I'd cleared the kitchen counter of little white takeout containers, paint chips, and Escalade brochures, I was refilling Jill's glass, again.

"I'm not so sure you should drive," I said, trying to sound innocent and sincere all the while calculating her drinks consumed to frisky ratio.

"If I couldn't before, I certainly won't be able to after this," she said, nodded then looked up at me and took a long sip.

She left sometime after 4:30 in the morning. It was still dark, or the last bit of dark, maybe just a pencil line of grey on the eastern horizon. I pulled my jeans on and walked her out to where her car was parked in front. We had a couple of long passionate kisses in the empty street, and a bit of a grope session before she climbed in and drove off.

There is something about the beginning of a relationship, when the only time you want to let go is to get a bigger handful of each other. Of course, you could probably say the same thing about a fight.

The temperature and humidity had dropped at least for the moment, but that smell was still in the air. I decided it might be a good idea to get back to sleep before my hangover had a chance to kick in. I swallowed two Tylenol tablets before I climbed back into bed. I slept where Jill had been, the bed still warm from her body, the covers frantic from our combined assaults, the pillow smelling of her perfume. I drifted off hoping for more sex in my dreams.

Chapter Thirty-Six

I could tell by the way the sun was frying the far side of the window shade that it was going to be another beastly day. I lay in bed and revisited my torrid late night with Jill. I rolled out of bed around noon and noticed her gold hoop earrings on the nightstand. Good, that meant she'd have to come back and get them.

I showered off the last of her perfume, dressed, made coffee, then gazed out the front window, sipping my first cup still thinking about last night. Not just the sex, but Mr. Swirlee as well. I had to find a way to get to him.

I half paid attention as a squad car pulled up across the street and parked. They'd glanced at my place. I didn't think much of it at first, but a minute or two later a second squad car arrived and parked directly in front of my house. One of the officers walked across the street and chatted with the guys in the first car. He looked back over at my place a couple of times as they talked. Something was up, and I didn't like it. I set my coffee down, grabbed my wallet, and walked out the back door.

That same smell was in the air, and a lot of flies. I wondered if I'd stepped in dog shit or something. I went over my back fence, walked across Mrs. Muller's yard and then down the street. By the time I'd reached the corner there was a squad car parked in front of the Muller house, two uniforms were walking up the driveway. I turned right and walked back on Arundel, looking to my right once I reached Selby. I was just three doors from my house.

There were four squad cars parked in front. Two uniforms stood on the porch at my front door. They were pounding loud enough that I could hear them as I stood on the corner. The rest, five officers, were gathered in the driveway, standing around my car.

I crossed Selby Avenue, then stopped and leaned against the corner of La Grolla, the restaurant directly across the street from my house and hoped I looked like an innocent bystander. The officers were discussing something, or a number of things. One of them, a sergeant, was continually talking on a radio. About ten minutes later a van arrived, white, City of St. Paul, Crime Scene Investigation Unit stenciled on the sides. On its heels came a hearse with a chrome plate in the side window that read Medical Examiner.

A man and a woman stepped into hazmat suits at the rear of the Crime Scene van. Once they were zipped in, they pushed a red, two-wheeled dolly up my driveway and proceeded to erect a small tent over my car. The cops were milling around. I could just make out snippets of nervous laughter. By now a half dozen curious people lingered on the street. A couple of people walking dogs stopped to watch the proceedings.

Another car pulled up, almost in front of me. A handmade sign, shirt cardboard and what looked like Magic Marker placed on the dashboard, POLICE.

Some baby-faced kid got out, needing a shave and wearing blue jeans and a T-shirt. He was carrying a video camera, a backpack, and had two more cameras around his neck.

This was not looking good.

The camera kid was greeted with more nervous laughter from a couple of cops. The guys on the front porch remained at my front door. I guessed they were past the point of hoping I might answer and were now waiting for a warrant to enter. I realized the smell I couldn't seem to shake all day yesterday wasn't from the river but from me, or at least my car. Garbage? Half right, rotting meat in this heat, or to be more precise, body. Someone was in the trunk of my car. I just had no idea who.

I didn't recognize any of the cops lingering a reasonable distance from the tent over my car. One young-looking guy, close cropped hair and muscles suddenly walked quickly away from the tent, down my driveway. He staggered a step or two, grabbed his knees, and then vomited in my front yard. He was followed by three or four other guys making a hasty retreat down the driveway. None of them got sick, but they clearly saw no reason to hang around my car any longer than necessary.

I guessed that meant they'd opened the trunk. Whoever was in there, it didn't matter at this point. The only thing that mattered just now was getting the hell out of here before someone recognized me. I was in serious trouble and for once I hadn't done anything to deserve it.

I started walking away, trying to think where I could go. Someplace I wouldn't be expected. Someplace I wasn't a regular. Someplace they wouldn't come looking for me. That left out a number of bars, Heidi, and probably Jill, too.

Chapter Thirty-Seven

I'd first met Tony Colli in the army, though I didn't know it at the time. Actually, it was during our final days, when we were mustering out. We'd been in Iraq at the same time, almost the same place, but only learned that in a later conversation. It was one of the little things that bound us, sort of.

The army, plus the fact he had been arrested, charged with murder, and was looking at a life sentence. I'd found the two women he had paid to be with the night he was supposed to have strangled a bank manager over in Wayzata. It didn't clear him absolutely, but was enough to raise doubt with a jury which eventually wouldn't convict him.

He went by the nickname Dog. He was the type of person you wouldn't call except as an absolute last resort. Not really the type of guy you wanted to see on a regular or even an irregular basis. He was Anthony to his mother and Dog to everyone else who knew him. Trouble seemed to follow Dog.

I didn't know exactly how to get in touch with him, but I knew who would. She wore her hair in a flaming red, tight perm. She was kind, gentle, wore too much lipstick, awful perfume, smoked nonstop,

150

weighed about three hundred pounds, and baked wonderful pies. Della Colli, Dog's mother.

"Hello, Mrs. Colli, this is Devlin Haskell."

"Who?"

"Devlin Haskell."

I'd taken the bus out to Como Park and was sitting on an out-of-the-way wooden bench, talking to Dog's mom on my cell phone. I was constantly looking around to make sure no one was paying attention to me.

"Oh, yes, Devlin. Why it's been so long. How are you?"

"Oh, just fine, thanks. How are you, Mrs. Colli?"

"Oh you know," a slight pause while she took a drag and then exhaled. "A few aches and pains, but at my age, the alternative is worse."

"Oh, Mrs. Colli, you'll outlive us all."

"Not if you behave," she said, I guess offering advice.

"Say, I've got some extra baseball tickets. I was thinking of Anthony, wondering if you had his number so I could give them to him."

"Oh, aren't you sweet. Why don't you give me your number and I'll have Anthony call you. He's so hard to get hold of nowadays."

No surprise. Dog was into something, again, and she was covering for him, again.

"Okay, you have a pen and paper?" I asked.

"Yes, go ahead, dear. I'm ready."

I gave her my phone number, we chatted for a minute or two longer before she'd suddenly had enough of me.

"Well, thank you. Anthony loves his baseball, so I'm sure he'll get back to you. I've got to run, good-bye, bye-bye," she said, hanging up, still talking as she did so.

There was only so much to do in a park with a small zoo while you're waiting for a phone call and trying to blend into the crowd. I looked at the tigers, fed the seals, stared at a number of young mommies. I thanked my lucky stars I didn't have to deal with screaming kids.

A few hours later I was sitting on a bench, watching the merry-go-round. Actually, to be more precise, I was catching the seductive smile of a blonde mommy every time she came around, riding up and down on a carved white unicorn. She wore white shorts, a tight aqua top and sandals. On her third pass she gave me a subtle little wave. As she came around the fifth time she grabbed the horn on the unicorn's head, raised her eyebrows, and gave me a little nod. On her sixth pass I had my back to her, talking to Dog.

"Dog, man, thanks for calling. I really need some help."

"Yeah, my mom said you're trying to get rid of some tickets to the ball game."

"What? No, not exactly. Look, here's the deal," I said, and then went on to explain about the smell from the day before, the police at my house and the body in my car. As I spoke, the background noise on the phone sounded as if he were calling from a bar.

When I'd finished, he said, "You're right, man, you're in some deep shit. You didn't kill this guy?" he asked, matter of fact, like a body in your trunk was just an occasional occurrence with everyone.

"No, I told you. I didn't kill anyone! Look, I don't know if it even was a guy. All I know is I'm pretty sure someone dumped a body in the trunk of my car. I got no idea who did it. I got no idea whose body it was.

152

I do know that there's a pretty good chance the police are looking for me. And, if they find me, I'll be locked up for a long damn time."

"So, what do you want me to do?" he said, not sounding like a jerk. He was making the offer I'd hoped for and desperately needed right now.

"First off, I need to get somewhere safe, somewhere I can try and sort all this out."

"This ain't the place," he said absently. "Tell me where you are. I'll come get you."

We arranged to meet a couple of blocks away in thirty minutes. I hung up, glancing around for the blonde on the unicorn. Like so many opportunities in life, she was gone almost as quickly as she had appeared.

Chapter Thirty-Eight

The Dog was one of those big guys. Not the sculpted bodybuilder type, more of a farm boy sort of big with heavy shoulders, chest, no neck, massive thighs and calves. He had wild dark hair that was always a mess and stood out in different directions. It was impossible to tell where his heavy black beard stopped and the body hair began. He seemed to be wrapped in wall-to-wall carpeting.

The bridge of his nose had been flattened in a number of different incidents over the years so that now just the tip popped out, like a thumb for hitchhiking. I wasn't sure he could even breathe out of the thing. It might be merely cosmetic.

He had huge hands, like bricks with sausage fingers and when I opened the door he reached over and yanked me inside his truck effortlessly.

If Dog was trying to keep a low profile, picking me up in a fire engine red Ram Charger with flames painted across the hood, a Confederate flag on the tailgate, and a hula girl on the dash, didn't seem to be a promising start. Still, he was here.

"What the hell happened to your head, man?" he asked, staring at my forehead.

"Man, Dog, can't thank you enough. When'd you get this thing?" I asked, ignoring his question as I settled in and buckled up.

"Oh, you know, just sort of picked it up."

Unfortunately, I did know. He sounded just a little too vague, and I glanced over at the ignition. It was torn out. The truck was stolen.

"Relax, relax," he said, catching the look of terror on my face. "From way down in southern Iowa, outside Ottumwa. No one up here is gonna be looking for the damn thing."

"Dog, normally not a problem, you know? I'm cool. It's just that, like I explained, my luck has really been running sort of horse shit lately, and I don't need any additional problems."

"Not to worry, bro, they'd have to catch us first." He laughed and then stomped on the accelerator.

"Dog, goddamn it, slow down, man. I'm trying to keep a low profile here, not end up on America's Most Wanted."

"Oh yeah, of course. I can dig it," he said, easing up on the gas. "Look, we're going out to my pad. Kind of laying low myself, if you know what I mean. Got a lake place," he added proudly.

Dog's idea of a lake place didn't really gel with mine. I was thinking water, waves, a dock, maybe a beach. God forbid females in tiny outfits sunning themselves and wanting cream rubbed all over their bodies.

Dog's place was more of a decrepit hunting shack on the backwater of a swamp. As we climbed out of the truck, I was struck by a high-pitched hum in the air. Mosquitoes, and lots of them.

"Better run for it. Fuckers get vicious this time of night," Dog said, taking off toward the shack. The ground shook as he ran for the wooden hovel. He yanked open the door. The screen was rusted, torn, and pulled back from the frame in a couple of different places.

Things weren't much better inside. There was a light on in the tiny kitchen, no more than fifteen watts. I guessed there was indoor plumbing because I could smell the bathroom.

"Hey, look, we can eat this shit," Dog said pushing his discovery toward me across the strip of rough, grease-coated plywood that served as the kitchen counter. It was a grimy pizza-delivery box with a receipt taped to the top of the box dated two days ago.

"Nah, with everything that's been going on I guess I'm not that hungry," I announced.

"Suit yourself, man." He shoved a triangle of congealed grease disguised as pizza between his teeth. With his two free hands he'd opened up a scuffed metal cooler on the floor. It was filled with murky water and five or six cans of beer. He pulled a can out and handed it to me over his shoulder, took one for himself, and kicked the lid closed with his boot.

"Shit. Have to go get some more. Didn't have room in the fridge so I just put some lake water in there to keep 'em, cool, ya know?"

Lake water?

I didn't care. Other than an overpriced hot dog at three and the fish I fed the seals I hadn't seen anything to eat or drink all day. I wasn't at the point where I'd risk eating the pizza, yet, but I figured any alcohol in the beer would kill the swamp germs.

Later that night I was sitting on the cooler, against the kitchen door, talking with Dog and trying to come up with a plan. Dog was sitting backward on a chair,

156

cleaning a subcompact Glock at a chipped enamel table with wobbly legs. He was able to reassemble the Glock without looking at what he was doing. He just kept talking to me, slipping the pieces back together. He worked the slide, shoved the clip back in, and then tucked the thing into the small of his back.

"Don't guess you got any firepower, do ya?"

"No." I shook my head.

"Well, sorry to piss in the punch bowl, but you're gonna need something. I got a 17 next to my bed. You can use that for the time being. Kind of big to cart around but she's better than nothing. Oh, which reminds me, you can flake out over there in the recliner." He nodded at what was left of an upholstered chair in the far corner in front of a shiny, new, forty-two-inch flat-screen TV.

I had a fear the flat screen came from the same place as the Ram Charger parked outside.

"I'll need your ass out of here tomorrow night. I got Noleen coming over." He raised his eyebrows, waiting for me to ask.

I felt like I had way too much information already.

"You can sleep in the truck if you want. We should see what we can do about a set of wheels for you. I can make a couple of calls."

"Yeah, I'd appreciate that, Dog."

"Seems to me, all the answers to your questions are with this Mr. Swirlee jackass. You get a hold of that son-of- a-bitch, and we'll get some answers for you."

"Yeah maybe. All I know is nothing is making any sense from this end. That's for damn sure."

"Well, don't feel all alone. We're in this together now, bro."

That was another thing worrying me.

Chapter Thirty-Nine

Between the incredibly uncomfortable recliner, Dog snoring in the tiny bedroom, things scurrying around inside the walls and mosquitoes, I didn't have what could be termed a restful night.

In the morning I turned my phone back on and checked for messages. There were eight.

Two from Heidi. "The police were just here. Where the hell are you? Call me if you're okay." The second message said, "Call me if you're not okay."

One was from Detective Manning. "Mr. Haskell, this is Detective Norris Manning with the St. Paul Police, homicide. It is imperative that you call me as soon as possible...blah, blah, blah, blah, blah."

Two from Aaron LaZelle. "Dev, Aaron, hey, give me a call. There's a heavy hammer about to fall on you. I can help. Call me, please." The second message said, "Just call, asshole, so I know you're okay."

Four messages from Jill. "Dev, hey, what's going on? The police were just here looking for you." The second message said, "Dev, give me a call. I'm really worried." The third message said, "If you're ignoring me I will kill you. Call me back." Her final message was slurred. I was guessing she was on about her fifth bottle of wine. From what I could make out she babbled and slurred her way through an explanation of how she didn't just jump into bed with anyone. Then she finished with, "So, just you never mind, because I'm not that kind of girl," she screamed. Her words became unintelligible from there, then silence that lasted for a couple of minutes until I got tired of listening and just deleted the message.

So there it was, the police were looking for me. Both of the women I hoped to take comfort in and/or with, were furious with me. And, I could look forward to spending the night sleeping in Dog's truck because some woman named Noleen, who clearly needed her head examined, was coming over to drink warm beer that had been sitting all day in a cooler full of swamp water.

Dog, amazingly, had been correct. All answers seemed to lie with Mr. Swirlee. I took the Glock 17 Dog had given me the night before, grabbed the screwdriver he used to start the truck and tip toed out while he was still snoring. It was time to get some answers from Mr. Swirlee.

Chapter Forty

It took me a few tries to get Dog's truck started, but I got it going. I drove to Mr. Swirlee's. Along the way I rehearsed lines and played a series of different scenarios in my head. I needn't have bothered. There were two squad cars parked out in front of the house. I drove past and kept right on going. If the police were here talking to Mr. Swirlee, there was a good chance they were also spending time with Heidi and Jill, as well. I drove down to the police station, parked on a side street, and returned Aaron's call.

"Where the hell are you?" he shouted just after the first ring.

"I'm around, don't worry." Figuring if they tried to triangulate where I placed my call from they'd think I was in the lobby of the station.

"Look, I don't know what happened, but you not coming in does nothing to help your situation. Where the hell are you? Let me come and get you, Dev."

"Aaron, I didn't know there was a body in my car."

"Okay, I believe you. Let me come and get you. We'll go over everything and get this figured out."

"You know it doesn't look good for me right now. I have to get some answers first."

"Dev, we want to hear your side, hear what you say happened. But hiding from us doesn't do a thing for you, except make you look even more guilty. So let me come and get you. Hey, we can even stop for coffee and I'll buy. What do you say?"

"Sounds tempting pal, but I have to get this figured out. It's just not making any sense, you know?"

"Yeah, I do know, Dev, and we're all here to help. Please, will you let me come and get you? We'll get this mess figured out. What do you say?"

"Just what I said before, nope, I gotta get a handle on this and at the end of the day there's only one guy who has all the answers."

"Who's that, Dev?"

"You kidding? You know, Mr. Swirlee."

"Mr. Swirlee?" he shouted, sounding incredulous.

"You got it he's the one guy who knows what the hell is going on."

There was a long pause. I could hear Aaron take a deep breath and then exhale.

"Look, Aaron, he's behind the fire-bombing of the Giant Scoop office. He's behind whoever tried to ram Jennifer McCauley off the High Bridge. He's tied into Bernie Sneen getting run over by that freight train. He's running shit out of his trucks. You know and I know it all comes back to Mr. Swirlee." It sounded so obvious as I said it out loud.

"Is that why we found him stuffed in your trunk?"

"What?"

"Mr. Swirlee, we found him in the trunk of your car, Dev."

"Are you sure?"

"Bald guy, carried a metal cane, left leg in a walking cast? He was beaten up pretty badly. Coroner says he was in there for a while before he died. Course this heat," he added absently.

"Are you telling me it was Mr. Swirlee's body in the trunk of my car?" I still had trouble believing it.

"Yeah, his wife reported him missing the day before. Look, I know you had some sort of dispute with him over money."

"He said he wouldn't pay my invoice."

"And you went over there, right? To his house? Broke in, threatened him, assaulted him, right?"

"Those charges don't tell the real story. They're bullshit, I..."

"Dev, I've seen the interview tape with Manning. Your face is bruised. You admit you were at the guy's house. I've read the report from the arresting officers. They state you were confused. Thought maybe you'd been drinking or taking drugs."

"Come on, Aaron, I wasn't drinking."

"Yeah, thank God you submitted to the Breathalyzer. But, your state of ..."

"Aaron, you ever know me to take drugs? Cut the bullshit," I yelled.

"Look, this isn't bullshit, pal. You are in trouble, big trouble. The guy filed charges against you then turned up dead in the trunk of your car with the shit kicked out of him and a plastic bag wrapped around his head. Hopefully, you can understand our concern and the desire to discuss a few things with you. Now, will you please let me help, Dev? Let me come and get..."

"I'll be in touch," I said and hung up.

Chapter Forty-One

Dog hadn't moved. He was still face down in bed snoring when I returned. Not a pretty sight. I sat in the recliner and thought for a long time, but didn't come up with anything new. Dog eventually rolled out of bed in the early afternoon, grunted a greeting, and set about cooking two pounds of bacon in the electric fry pan that served as his stove. I was hoping he might think about a shirt to wear with his boxer shorts while he was cooking, but the thought didn't seem to cross his mind.

"Jesus Christ, no offense, man, but you look even worse than last night when you were moaning your ass off around here," he said.

I was leaning against the plywood counter.

He set a grease soaked paper plate piled high with bacon strips between us then delicately picked up one of the strips with his fingertips.

"Fuck, that's hot, man," he said, then stuffed the thing in his mouth, sucking in air in an effort to cool it down as he turned his head from side to side.

"Jesus," I said.

"Look." He gasped through a mouthful of bacon. "I told you last night we just go get your buddy

Swirlee. You'll have your answers pretty damn quick, I promise." He swallowed and quickly crammed two more pieces into his mouth. "This shit's good, man. Better grab some, 'fore it's all gone."

I reached for a piece, held it upright, took a bite, and chewed.

"We can't talk to Swirlee."

"Why the hell not?"

"Cause it turns out it was his body in the trunk of my car."

"No shit? Thought you told me you didn't…"

"I didn't. I have no idea how in the hell he got in there."

"How'd you find out?"

"Talked to a cop pal. He says they figure Swirlee was stuffed in there alive. At least for a while, before he died. Someone wrapped a plastic bag around his head."

Dog was reading my mind.

"So it looks like you beat the shit out of the guy, stuffed him in your trunk, and he wakes up dead, right?"

I nodded.

"You been set up, man. By someone who is pretty damn good. He have a wife? Even with a name like Swirlee?" Dog chuckled at his joke then stuffed more bacon in his mouth.

"Yeah. Well, no. I mean, I thought she was his wife. Turns out she's just the girlfriend, but I don't have any…"

"She'll do. Knock off the negative-vibe shit, Dev. She's the one. Odds are she did it. You should know this stuff. You're supposed to be the big private eye, aren't you? Seems pretty obvious to me."

"Look…"

164

"Look, nothing. Let me give you the scenario, here. She's pretty hot, right? The old man has all the dough. She sits around all day in the sun or just goes shopping, probably has a boyfriend on the side. The old man is a pain in her ass so she has the boyfriend take the guy out. Sound about right?"

"No, not really."

"As far as you know, but that don't mean shit. No, look at the girlfriend. Now, we just gotta find a way to nail her. Or, blackmail the bitch. Get one of those revenue streams going that rich folks are always talking about." He stuffed two more pieces of bacon into his mouth. "It's so obvious, man. Think about it," he said, spitting bacon bits across the kitchen.

Chapter Forty-Two

I was still thinking about it later that night. I was stretched out across the seat of Dog's truck, parked about thirty feet from the cabin when Noleen arrived a little before nine. She pulled up in a rust-flecked Geo Metro, with dents in every quarter panel and a cracked windshield. It had probably been red, originally, but over the ensuing fifteen plus years it had aged to a flat, dark pink. The brakes wheezed and ground the car to a halt.

She stepped out, scratched, exhaled a cloud of smoke, then flicked her cigarette against the side of the cabin. She had long hair that looked too black. It had been colored so that even a guy like me, lying in the front seat at twilight, could spot it from thirty feet as a bad dye job. If she noticed me lying in the truck she didn't pay any attention.

She wore blue jean cutoffs, unfortunately a couple of sizes too small. A light blue T-shirt rested just a little too high and exposed her midsection. Pale flesh on her substantial belly and love handles jiggled over the waist band of her cutoffs. She carried a large brown purse on her right shoulder and a half empty bottle of Jack Daniels in her left hand. She'd been drinking, which seemed to me like a good idea, given what she was headed for. She didn't knock, just opened the torn screen door and walked in.

They laughed, yelled, screamed, and moaned until sometime after three in the morning. I would wake up periodically, start the truck, let the air conditioner cool things down, then drift off to a sweaty, fitful sleep. At least until the heat from the night or noise from the loving couple awoke me again.

I was still asleep about eleven thirty the following morning when Dog suddenly opened the passenger door in the truck, then caught me before I tumbled out backwards.

"Hey, time for me to give Noleen a lift home. I squared it with her so you can use her car for a couple of days," he said. His eyes were bloodshot, and he stood there barefoot, no shirt, waiting for me to get out of the truck.

"You okay to drive?" I asked, climbing out. He ignored my question, stumbled around to the driver's side, and hopped in.

Noleen stood at the back of the truck, holding onto the tailgate. She gave me the semblance of a wave, but I don't think she really saw anything further than six inches beyond her nose. She had her T-shirt on, minus a bra. Her cutoffs were inside out. She fell down on her first attempt to climb into the cab.

I rushed over to help her up.

"No, no, don't. Get away, I'm okay," she mumbled, then waved me off before she crawled in and closed the door behind her.

Dog gave me a nod and then spun away, churning up dirt and gravel as he drove off.

It was hard to believe the inside of the place could be messier than normal, but it was. The wobbly kitchen table lay at a sharp angle. The two chrome legs at one end had broken off. Noleen's Jack Daniels bottle was empty, on its side and pushed up against a wall. Beer cans were littered across the floor. An empty plastic vodka bottle sat on the floor next to the recliner. A half-finished bottle of peppermint schnapps lay on its side in a sticky puddle in the middle of the plywood kitchen counter. A thong the size of a water balloon slingshot hung from a closet doorknob. I was afraid to touch anything.

I rescued Noleen's car keys from the pool of peppermint schnapps and rinsed them off in the sink. Five minutes later the Geo rumbled and groaned to life and I drove off. If I couldn't get the answers from Mr. Swirlee, I figured I would get them from Lola. Much as I hated to admit it, Dog was probably right. Odds were she did it.

Chapter Forty-Three

The police cars were gone from the front of Mr. Swirlee's house, but the two attack dogs lounged on the front steps pretending to sleep, no doubt hoping to lure some innocent through the front gate as a midday snack. Under the circumstances, I didn't think ringing the doorbell would be the best idea. I pulled around the corner, ground the brakes to a stop, then settled in to keep an eye on the alley and Mr. Swirlee's garage.

While waiting for the next four hours I searched Noleen's car. Along with bags from a number of fast-food joints and two condom wrappers, I found a little airline bottle of vodka. On the floor of the passenger side was a sales receipt for $49.95, dated yesterday, from a shop called the Love Doctor. On the floor of the back seat there was a tube of prescription cream with directions to "apply four times daily to the infected area until rash no longer exists." I'd have to let Dog know.

A little after six the garage door opened, and Lola drove out in the black Mercedes CL600. She turned out of the alley and drove right past me. Fortunately, she was distracted by her cell-phone conversation and didn't notice me. I cranked the Geo to life and followed her at a distance.

She drove for about ten minutes over to a building with 'Mr. Swirlee' written in pink-and-blue script letters across the front. Next to that hung the giant Mr. Swirlee ice cream logo. She stopped partially across the sidewalk, in front of a garage door until it opened automatically and she drove in.

I drove past, made a U-turn two blocks down, then pulled to the curb and waited. I didn't wait long. Lola drove out of the garage and back down the street. She didn't back out, which suggested the garage was fairly large. Coming out of the garage almost immediately behind her was a large, black vehicle. A Hummer, an H3x to be exact. Not a cheap mode of transport. Despite the headrests, I could see three large heads silhouetted as they followed her down the street.

She drove to a bank and parked in the lot. The Hummer pulled alongside, and a guy climbed out. He had a large, round, shaved head with a black mustache. I could just make out his earrings and the splotch of blue tattoo on the back of his hands. I recognized him as the bald jackass who had held the shotgun on me. The same guy working the betting station in the ice cream truck the night I got sucker-punched. He was dressed in cowboy boots, trousers, T-shirt, all black over a fairly muscled body.

I wrote down both license plate numbers on a McDonald's bag.

Baldy walked over to the driver's side of the Mercedes. Lola lowered the window no more than three or four inches. Just low enough to cram a purple nylon bag into the bald thug's waiting paws. As soon as he took the bag she raised the window. No words seem to be exchanged.

170

The moment he placed the bag into the night-deposit drop, she put the Mercedes in gear and drove off. The Hummer waited as he climbed back in, then sped up to follow her home. They all turned down the side street to get to the alley. I continued straight so they wouldn't spot me, then doubled back. The Geo brakes ground to a noisy stop as I pulled over to watch the alley. I sat there until about ten thirty that night, then left. I decided to drive over to Jill's house rather than call, but when I arrived there was a car parked in front. I didn't want to risk running into someone or putting Jill in an uncomfortable position, so I left and drove over to Heidi's.

I noticed the rear kitchen light was on as I drove past. If she was out she always left the front entry light on, just to alert would-be burglars that the house was empty. I parked, walked down the alley and into her backyard. I could see her drinking a glass of wine, sitting at her kitchen counter and watching something that looked like American Idol or Biggest Loser on the flat screen, highbrow stuff. She appeared to be alone.

As I walked up the back steps a light automatically flashed on. I knocked softly on her back door.

"Who is it?" she called a moment or two later.

"It's me, Dev, open up," I said, then glanced around nervously. I was standing directly under the spotlight illuminating her entire yard.

"What do you want?" she asked.

"Heidi, damn it, open up, come on!"

I heard the lock snap and she opened the door.

"Can I come in? Christ, I'm getting eaten alive out here."

She stood to one side so I could enter, then locked the door behind me.

"Just what the hell have you done? And where in the hell have you been? I've been trying to reach you for a couple of days. Do you have any idea how worried I've been?"

It was Heidi at her most dangerous. Eyes tearing up and flashing at the same time, bottom lip quivering, and she was standing next to the knife rack.

"I got all that cleared up, don't worry," I tried to sound casual.

"Cleared up? Don't worry? Is that why you're sneaking around to my back door? What the hell's going on? The police have been here, twice."

"Just a little misunderstanding, I…"

"Misunderstanding! Hey, I posted bail for you. You didn't have any problem calling me that night, did you? I'm on the hook for about five grand here. Misunderstanding! You can't just blow me off like that, Dev."

"Okay, okay, could you stop screeching for a minute so I can get a word in edgewise and explain things?" I said, groveling for time, trying to think of what I was going to say.

"Explain things…oh, please, do. Go on," she said, then cocked her hips and crossed her arms. Not a good sign.

"Okay, look…Mr. Swirlee…I told you a little about him. Turns out things got a bit more complicated. Hey, you got any beer in the fridge?"

"Oh, God, help yourself. Christ, I'll need some more of that wine, too. So…Mr. Swirlee…you were saying."

I went on to tell her most of the facts. Jill's fire, Jennifer McCauley's crash, Bernie Sneen's final train ride, Swirlee not paying my invoice, assaulting me, and finally his body stuffed and baking in the trunk of

172

my car. I left out the part about Jill spending the night, Lola hitting on me, and the suntan oil.

"Detective Manning failed to mention any of that," she said. We were sitting on her living room couch by now. I was doing my best to make sure her wine glass was never empty.

"Manning, that guy's just out to nail me. I don't know what his problem is," I said.

"Well, it might have something to do with a body and the fact that the victim filed charges against you just the day or two before. Charges, I might add, that I posted bail so you…"

"Yeah, I get that, but he's just not looking at the facts here. For starters," I began, and then it dawned on me. "For starters, I think I was in police custody when I was supposed to have put Mr. Swirlee in the trunk of my car. I think I may have been locked up."

"What do you mean?"

"I mean, the best thing you might have done for me was continue on with your evening of debauchery while I spent the night locked up in police custody."

"Oh brother." She chuckled, but then took another sip and gave me that smile that suggested she was feeling no pain.

Chapter Forty-Four

I felt so guilty at seven the following morning when Heidi kissed me good-bye and tiptoed off to work that I snuggled down and slept for another hour and a half. The place was clean, rodent free, with a full refrigerator and Heidi with benefits. I showered, then sat at her kitchen counter drinking coffee and picking at a Hostess Twinkie, wondering what the hell I was going to do.

An hour later I was still wondering the same thing while I sat parked at the end of Swirlee's alley. I was waiting for Lola and her band of scary men to go somewhere so I could follow. And then what?

"Haskell Investigations," I answered after failing to read Jill's name on my caller ID.

"Oh, God, Dev, finally. Are you okay?"

"Me? Yeah sure, how are things going?"

"How are things going? Forget that. What happened? The police have been here a couple of times asking about you. I'm hearing awful reports. What's going on?"

"Actually, just a little misunderstanding," I said, trying to down play Swirlee's murder. The garage door was going up, and Lola drove off down the alley. A moment later the Hummer pulled out and followed her.

I started the Geo, or at least tried to.

"Come on, damn it," I said by way of encouragement.

"You okay? And what's that terrible noise?" Jill asked as the car suddenly gasped to life, farting a grey cloud of exhaust into the air.

"Oh, sorry, I was walking past a cement mixer and the guy just turned the thing on, I couldn't hear you at all."

"Sounded awful," she said as the Geo lurched down the alley in pursuit.

"Yeah, I can't imagine putting up with that all day. Course, you had those bells," I added, wishing I could have pulled the words back the moment they crossed my lips.

"Yeah," she said sadly, then silence.

"So, the police paid you a visit?" I accelerated through a yellow light and then backed off.

"Yeah, they were asking about you. Well, and Mr. Swirlee. I told them I didn't know anything, which is pretty much the truth. But then I called you a couple of times and never heard anything back."

"Yeah, I had the phone turned off. You know, working with the police, trying to get this whole mess sorted out. I just listened to your messages last night, but I thought it might be too late to call," I lied, not adding, plus I was climbing into Heidi's orgy-sized bed.

"So then, everything is cleared up?"

"Just about, a couple of loose ends, but nothing serious," I said. Lola and the three goons had pulled over in front of a brick warehouse. She got out of her car once the goons were standing around her. The three of them provided some pretty tight security looking up, down, and across the street, then glancing five stories up toward the rooftop before they made their way to the door, a phalanx, Lola protected in the middle.

"…later tonight?"

"What? I'm sorry, my phone cut out there, I missed what you said," I recovered, still wondering what in the hell Lola and her thugs were up to.

"I asked, are you interested in coming over for dinner tonight? Say about seven-thirty?"

"This isn't going to prompt a call later on about you not being that type of girl, is it?" I joked.

"What?"

With that one word, if she was faking it, she was doing a damn good job. She clearly didn't remember the final drunken phone message she'd left me. Bringing it up now would not do one thing to increase my chances. There were only three words to describe my question. Stupid, stupid, stupid!

"I'll see you around seven-thirty. What can I bring?"

"Not a thing. Let's make it a very special celebration in honor of you getting things cleared up."

"I like the sound of that," I said.

"I mean it, I've got something really special planned, for both of us," she said. I could feel my phone heating up as she spoke.

"See you tonight, seven-thirty," I said.

"Counting on it." She sounded almost breathless.

Chapter Forty-Five

I waited down the block for a few more hours.

A half hour after Lola and the goons entered. A total of five other cars had arrived, all separately. I had no idea if they were related to whatever Lola was involved in. They were all driven by guys you wouldn't give a second look to if you passed them on the street. None of them even remotely gave the appearance of the security theatrics Lola and her friends had displayed.

By now it was close to the end of the workday. The streets were getting busier with people adding to rush hour. Parked for the afternoon a block away in the wretched little Geo I'd dosed off half a dozen times. Every time I had jerked awake the cars were still in position.

Eventually I came to and saw one of Lola's goons, the dopey looking guy with the crew cut, standing out in front of the building. He looked a little nervous, and seemed to fidget while talking to himself as he paced back and forth on the sidewalk. After five or six minutes he went back inside the building.

I caught the unmistakable sound of gunfire. There's only one thing that sounds like that. Not firecrackers or doors slamming or hammers pounding. I knew exactly what it was. There was a single shot, then after a couple of seconds it was followed by three or four more, then the loud, ripping burst of an automatic weapon.

Suddenly something flew through a glass window on the third floor. I could see the guy's legs moving back and forth like he was running as he hurtled through the air toward the ground. He landed on the sidewalk and bounced visibly as shards of glass rained and tinkled around him. Then he lay very still on the sidewalk in an unnatural, crumpled position. Almost immediately the goon who had been pacing back and forth flew out the door of the building, jumped in the Hummer and started it up.

More shots sounded from inside the building. I made out some single shots, then a pause before I heard another rip from an automatic weapon. The front door flew open again. This time it was the two goons with Lola. Lola was running barefoot, holding her heels and a large grocery bag.

She ran to her car, screaming something to one of the goons. He fired a round into the head of the body lying on the sidewalk, then slammed the Hummer door closed and the two vehicles rocketed down the street and screeched around a corner.

I cranked the key in the Geo, then cranked some more, again, and again. Finally, it sprang to life, but there was no way I was going to be able to catch up with Lola. I raced up to where their cars had been parked and cautiously got out, watching the shattered third-floor window as I made my way to the figure on the sidewalk. Dark blood pooled around the body and spread across the concrete. I felt for a pulse but didn't find one. I reached in the guy's rear pocket, and pulled out his wallet.

Someone suddenly shouted from the shattered window.

"Hey, what the hell are you doing?"

He waved a pistol, then fired wide. I heard the round slap into the side of the Geo. I pulled the Glock and fired back. I wasn't thinking, I just fired at the body mass in the window, two rounds, maybe three. The guy sort of grunted or coughed, then dropped from sight. I didn't bother to wait around, just jumped back into the Geo and drove off. I clanked my way around the corner, aware that there were a number of people out on the street watching me.

Chapter Forty-Six

I took a very roundabout way back to Dog's
place. I used side streets and back county roads,
making sure I wasn't being followed. I was worried
that not only had someone given my description to the
police, they may have gotten the license number to the
Geo as well.

It was dark by the time I arrived. I examined the
bullet hole in the passenger door, about all you could
say was it had missed the window. I doubted Noleen
would ever notice.

Dog wasn't there, and if the state of the place was
any indication, he hadn't returned since he drove off
with Noleen the other morning. Everything was still an
absolute mess. About the only difference was that the
puddle of Peppermint schnapps had soaked into the
plywood counter, mixing with the grease already there
to make an attractive sticky mess for the large blue
flies crawling and buzzing about.

Just to do something else, I set about cleaning the
place. Amazingly, there were cleaning supplies stored
beneath the kitchen sink. Not surprisingly, they
consisted of an unopened jug of Mr. Clean, a full can

of cleanser along with a sponge still wrapped in plastic and a bucket.

By midnight I had sort of calmed down. Dog's shack was beginning to resemble less of a hazardous waste site and more of a place modestly fit for human habitation. I turned on the flat screen, and watched a repeat of the ten o'clock news. It led with the story of, to quote, "Murder and mayhem, as shots rang out in the warehouse district of St. Paul earlier this evening."

The news report, taking up eight of the fifteen minutes dedicated to news, went on to list two men dead. A third was hospitalized in critical condition with multiple gunshot wounds. They gave the standard, 'police are asking that anyone with information contact them', appeal. The report then went on to describe a "small, dark maroon vehicle, driven by a Caucasian male, with the letters VJI or possibly VJL on the license plate." The driver was to be considered armed and dangerous.

I went outside to check. Noleen's license plate read VJL 775. Now what? It was then that I remembered Jill's dinner invitation.

It was too late to call her. And what would I say after having told her everything but a few loose ends were tied up.

I opened the wallet I'd taken off the guy on the sidewalk. The license read Roger Ackerman, which sort of rang a bell, but I couldn't place it.

I decided going to bed might be the better idea, so I settled into the recliner and closed my eyes.

Dog came in about three in the morning and shook me.

"What the hell happened?" he asked.

I was going to tell him I was just following Lola when all hell broke loose. Some guy jumped or was thrown through the window, another guy shot at me, Lola and the goons drove off. But then he followed up with,

"Fucking place smells like a Christmas tree."

"That would be the Mr. Clean. I sort of tidied up a bit." Apparently he hadn't noticed the three large green trash bags leaning up against the outside of the place. I didn't mention them.

"You shouldn't have bought all that shit."

"I didn't. You had it under the sink. That's where the cleaning supplies are."

"They are?" He sounded generally perplexed as he scratched his thigh, then grimaced a little.

"Dog, would I kid you? Hey listen, this afternoon there…"

"Look, before you get to that…sorry, but Noleen needs her wheels back. She's gotta go see her sister or some bullshit up north."

"My ma, I already told ya's," someone screeched from the kitchen area. I glanced around Dog, and there stood Noleen, same cutoffs, different T-shirt. She had a glass to her lips, with about an inch of what I guessed was peppermint schnapps. She tossed it back, then smiled.

"Anyway, you got them keys? She wants to take off now," Dog said, ignoring her.

"Now?"

"You got the keys?" He scratched again.

I handed over the keys and thanked Noleen. She pounded down a second glass of peppermint schnapps before she raced out the door and drove away. I figured the car hidden up in the Minnesota wilderness couldn't hurt my cause any.

"God, she can be a pain in the ass," Dog said, then made a face as her taillights disappeared over a distant rise.

"What's wrong with you?"

"I got this burn, like a sunburn or something on my crotch, man."

"I think I got just the thing for you," I said, going back inside. I grabbed Noleen's prescription cream lying underneath the wallet I'd taken from the dead guy on the sidewalk. Then proceeded to fill Dog in on just how my day had gone.

"Any money in the wallet?" he asked.

"I didn't think to check. Just read the driver's license is all. Roger Ackerman."

Dog took a long time to say something.

"You don't think that's Pinky Ackerman? What'd he look like?"

"Not too sure, other than bloody and very dead. Then some guy took a shot at me, so I fired back a couple of times before I got the hell out of there."

"No shit." He sounded impressed. "You got two rounds off at the guy. Think you hit him?"

"I don't know, not my top concern right now. I need to know what was going on there. I'm convinced this Lola is tied into something really big and really bad. I'm more positive than ever she's the one who stuffed that body in my car. What I can't figure out is why?"

"Told ya it was the chick, man," Dog replied.

A couple of beers bathed in swamp water and another hour of discussion did nothing to clear anything up.

Chapter Forty-Seven

I was up around nine. A few fitful hours in Dog's recliner had done nothing to improve my outlook. I felt like a bent piece of plumbing pipe. Dog was up shortly after that, looking none the worse given his activity for the past couple days. But then how could you really tell?

"First thing we gotta do is get you some wheels," he said spitting bacon across the floor that I had cleaned last night.

"Think Noleen made it up north?"

"Probably, less she passed out behind the wheel somewhere along the way. She left here about three-thirty so I'd put her in the deep woods a little after seven this morning. Hell, she's on a damn logging trail by now. Might be a good idea to keep an eye peeled for a day or so, but I wouldn't worry too much. Besides, not like she knows your name. Cops come, just deny that shit. Course you got a couple of bigger problems."

"Oh yeah, those."

Dog placed a few calls and late that morning got a call back. We were watching a black-and-white movie from I guess about 1955. Some detective thing that was moving painfully slow. I could say I listened to one side of his phone conversation, but that would suggest there had been a conversation.

When his phone rang Dog had turned down the volume with the remote. He answered the phone with a grunt, then held up his end of the conversation with more grunts. After about ninety seconds he gave a final grunt and hung up.

"Let's go get your wheels, man," he said turning off the flat screen. We climbed into his truck. As sort of an afterthought Dog said,

"Oh yeah, this'll run ya about twenty-five hundred."

"Twenty-five hundred?!" I gasped as we bounced onto the main road.

Dog glanced over at me with a sense of disbelief.

"Yeah, twenty-five hundred. It was a rush job. Hell, it probably took 'em five or six hours just to get the thing down here."

"What?"

"The car. Your car. You know, so you can drive around and figure all this shit out, instead of just capping that broad like I would. What? You think I'm gonna be your damn chauffer or something?"

"Look, Dog, I…I don't have twenty-five hundred bucks, just for starters. I'm sure it's a great deal and all that, but I don't have that sort of cash."

He gave a long sigh, and shook his head disgustedly.

"Walter ain't the kind of guy you stiff or tell 'catch you later'. How much can you come up with?"

"I'm sort of close to running on empty," I said.

"Oh, God. Okay, okay, I'll cover ya, but you gotta get it back to me, man."

"Yeah, thanks I appreciate that Dog. Really I do, but well, about this car, what…"

"Ahhh, shit, don't go getting all legal and everything on me, okay? You need some wheels, I got you some. A step up from Noleen's piece of shit, I might add. Look, no need to thank your buddy here for going out on a limb for ya. Just forget it. We'll get the damn car. The deal is no questions asked, got it?"

I really wasn't in a position to argue so I just nodded.

"Smart boy," Dog said.

Chapter Forty-Eight

We met the prospective seller, Walter, in the Trend bar. Walter was a black man with close-cropped hair and skin the color of milky tea. He was nicely dressed in slacks, a dark blue polo shirt, shiny, comfortable-looking black loafers, and what looked like a very expensive watch. He sat at the bar nursing a cup of coffee. It was just a little past noon and the place was packed, although no one crowded Walter.

As we entered there was a noticeable drop in casual conversation. All eyes followed us until Dog spoke to Walter, whereupon the noise level returned.

The transaction took no more than a minute. Dog palmed a roll of cash into Walter's hand. Between sips of coffee Walter gave Dog the vehicle location, across the street in the Rainbow Food parking lot as it turned out. The key would be waiting for us under the floor mat on the driver's side.

Back outside, standing on the street in front of the bar, Dog said, "Look, you get the car, come on back to my place. A couple of Big Macs for your buddy here might not be a bad idea. You can cover that much, can't ya?"

"You don't want to see the car?"

"What difference would it make? Besides, if someone was gonna nail you, that car would be as good a place as any. So no, I don't need to be there. See you back at the lake, right?"

"The lake," I nodded.

"And don't forget them Big Macs," Dog called as he climbed into his truck.

My new vehicle was a silver Buick Regal. After chugging around in Noleen's Geo it looked like something James Bond might drive, except for the North Dakota license plate, chromed wheel covers, a leather interior, and less than twelve thousand miles on the odometer. The phrase, *interstate transportation of stolen goods* sprung immediately to mind.

The driver's side door was unlocked and beneath the floor mats were two shiny new chrome keys. I was able to start the car without ear-splitting alarms going off, then pulled into a nearby McDonald's to pick up Dog's lunch.

Back at the lake and through a mouth crammed full of Big Mac, Dog reiterated his version of my options.

"Follow this broad and wait for her to fuck up, then call the cops, seeing as how you won't handle certain aspects on your own."

I couldn't argue with his logic.

"One other thing," I said. "I've got the license number of Lola's Mercedes and the Hummer those Neanderthals are driving…"

"They're brothers? That's their name?" As he spoke, Dog spit Big Mac and fries in my general direction.

"No, it's not their name, just a term. Look, I got the license numbers. Just call the cops from a pay phone, don't use your cell. Tell them you saw the cars

188

at the shooting yesterday. Give a description and make sure you give them the license numbers. Make it sound like you don't want to get involved. Hopefully someone else called in and mentioned the same thing and didn't pay attention to me in that bomb of Noleen's."

"You can count on me to be the good citizen," Dog said.

Chapter Forty-Nine

After lunch Dog went off to make his phone call. I settled into the recliner and took a nap. When I woke up I turned my cell phone on to check for messages. There was one from Detective Manning, two from Aaron and seven from Jill.

Manning's message was pretty straight-forward.

"Mr. Haskell, I'm advising you to surrender to law enforcement authorities...blah, blah, blah."

Both of Aaron's were a little more to the point.

"You fucking idiot. Call me, damn it!"

"Dev, you're running out of time. Don't screw this up. Call me, you dipshit."

Jill's started out sounding rational, but eventually went off the deep end.

"Hi, Dev, Jill here. Almost eight o'clock. Hope you didn't forget our date. Give me a call. Bye."

"Hey Dev, this is Jill. It's about eight fifteen. No problem, but you're starting to worry me. Please call."

"Dev, Jill. You were supposed to be here an hour ago. You okay?"

"Dev, don't come over. Call me...please."

"What the hell is it with you? At least call for God's sake!"

"Don't ever call me, ever! Do you hear! Ever!"

"Fuck you!"

The last message had been left a little after midnight and pretty much summed things up. Ironic that I was where I was, due in some part because I had gotten involved with Jill. At least on a client level. Now two people were dead, I was hiding from the police on a murder charge and driving a stolen car with North Dakota plates. Perfect.

There was only one person who could help me, and so I called her.

"Hello."

"Lola, Dev Haskell."

"What do you want?"

"I thought we should get together and chat."

"I really have nothing to say to you. Except to tell you that the police are looking for you." She spit out the last word, implying the mere mention of me was distasteful.

"Really? Is that because they found something in my car?" I asked.

"You are a cruel bastard, you know that? I plan to see that you get exactly what you have coming. If you so much…"

"Oh, you must be referring to your precious Mr. Swirlee. Yeah funny thing. I've got an alibi. A pretty good one as it turns out. Wanna hear?"

"I have no idea what you're talking about."

"That is probably the only honest thing you've said to me."

"What do you mean, alibi?"

"Well, it's just that when someone stuffed your little love toy, Mr. Swirlee, into the trunk of my car, to make it look like I did it, guess what? I was safely locked up in a jail cell."

191

"Locked up in jail? That doesn't surprise me, but I don't see what that has to do with me. It's something for the authorities to deal with, and believe me, they're going to hear about this phone call just as soon as I hang up."

"Good, while you're talking with them, you might mention the shooting at the warehouse yesterday. Two dead. Interesting, and you running out barefoot, carrying your heels with everything in a shopping bag, that was…"

"I…I don't know what in the hell you're taking about."

"Oh, okay. I just thought it might benefit both of us if you wanted to discuss the situation. But apparently you don't. Look, you go ahead and call the cops, because when you're done I'm going to have a nice chat with them and I think they'll find my story a little more interesting. What do you think?"

"I…I think you're nuts, crazy. What did you want to talk about, anyway?"

"Maybe what it would take to get me to just go away."

"Go away?"

"Yeah. Everyone has a price, even me."

"I can only imagine. Not that I give a damn, but what would your price be?"

"That's why we should talk. I tell you what. Why don't you plan on meeting me in a nice public place, tomorrow."

"Why not tonight? Maybe double your pleasure?" she said, suddenly eager to get together.

"Tonight, well, I can think of a couple of reasons. It would be dark, for one. And, the fact that I don't trust you comes to mind, but actually, I've already got plans for tonight. So, I'll call you tomorrow. Oh, one more thing. I'm going to tell you to come alone, so leave your bodyguards at home, okay?"

"Maybe you'd be a little more agreeable if I…"

I hung up and switched my phone off.

Chapter Fifty

I phoned Dog, and arranged to meet him about midnight at The Spot where I explained my plan, such as it was, over a couple of beers. We were sitting in a booth, just the two of us. One thing about being somewhere with Dog, no one wanted to join you.

"I don't know. Why don't you just take them all out? No hassle, long as no one sees you," he said shaking his head.

"Yeah, and no way to beat the rap for Swirlee's body ending up in the trunk of my car. He could have been in there for days with that plastic bag wrapped around his head. Hell, I don't know," I said, then washed down my concern with more beer.

"Oh, yeah, that."

"Look. I'm meeting her, Lola, tomorrow. But tonight I need your help in dealing with her bodyguards. They'll all be somewhere in the vicinity of that ice cream truck, running their betting shop. If we could take care of them there…"

"Blow them away?" Dog asked. He almost sounded hopeful.

"No, I think it would be best if no one was killed here, Dog. But maybe if we could just get them out of the way, say for a day, possibly two. We can nail darling Lola and then turn the whole bunch over to the cops."

"Maybe I forgot to mention it, but I've been sort of keeping a low profile around the cops, lately," Dog replied, knowing full well he had mentioned it.

"That's the beauty of this. We deliver this scum to the police on a platter, they wipe away the phony charges against me and the stuff against you. It's simple. We can cut a deal," I said, sort of half believing it.

Dog didn't look all that convinced.

"I still think it would be easier to just blow them all away."

"Look, can we just do this my way, please?"

"Yeah sure, why not? You've certainly done well up to this point."

Chapter Fifty-One

At 2:25 that morning I sat in the front seat of
Dog's Ram Charger, watching the Mr. Swirlee's ice
cream truck from a block away. We'd left my new car
at The Spot. It was after closing, and the streets had
gotten pretty quiet downtown. The black Hummer was
parked across the street, maybe twenty feet back from
the ice cream truck.

"Let's just keep it simple. I'll walk up to the ice
cream truck like I'm gonna place a bet. The guy has a
shotgun with him in there. I hold my gun on him," I
said.

"Then what?"

"That brings Tweedle Dumb and Tweedle Dumber
out. Soon as you see them walking across the street
you drive up behind, and get the drop on them. We got
all three. Easy. No one gets hurt."

"You say so." Dog sounded dejected.

"Yeah, it has to go down like this, otherwise we
find ourselves in a lot more trouble. Use these plastic
ties to cuff them. We'll pile them all into the Hummer
and bring 'em back to the lake. Sound like a plan?"

"Whatever, let's just get her done," Dog groaned.

I walked down the street, trying to act as casual as possible with a Glock 17 stuffed in my belt. I only hoped the thugs in the Hummer didn't recognize me before I got the draw on Baldy in the truck.

"Hey, how's it going?" I asked, approaching the window.

It was the same guy, bald, muscular, mustache, dressed all in black. The blue glare coming from his laptop reflected off his large bald head. He sort of looked like a full moon floating inside the darkened ice cream truck. He half grunted an acknowledgement.

"Still taking action on the All Star game?" I asked.

"Hell, yes, Jesus, it ain't for another two…"

My Glock suddenly resting in the middle of the window cut the rest of his conversation off.

"Don't think about doing anything stupid. Put your hands on top of that fat, bald head. Now just sit there real still like, and we'll wait for your two pals."

He raised his hands up onto his head, his biceps bulged, his forearms looked like logs, and I was awfully glad I had the Dog nearby to keep things calm.

"Hey, you're that fuck…"

"Shut up!" I snarled then waited for the approach of his pals.

It took another minute or two before they came. Unfortunately, they started the Hummer, flicked the headlights on then drove across the street toward me. I started glancing back and forth, from Baldy to the Hummer gaining speed, back to Baldy. The Hummer was almost there.

"Don't!" I yelled, keeping the Glock trained on him as he started to move. He thought better of it.

The Hummer suddenly accelerated.

I dropped, got just a half roll out of the way before it slammed into the side of the ice cream truck where I had been standing a second before. The truck rocked and skidded sideways a couple of feet. I heard things crashing about inside, glass breaking. Baldy groaned and then seemed to be coughing. As I scrambled to my feet the glow from the laptop was gone. There was something electric zapping and sizzling from inside the truck.

The Hummer pulled backward. The right side headlights were smashed. As it screeched to a stop I was aware of glass tinkling onto the street. Something seemed to be dragging from the wheel well on the passenger side and scraping the pavement. Suddenly the engine roared and the Hummer lurched forward.

I heard the unmistakable sound of a shotgun round being chambered behind me. I jumped just as the Hummer slammed into the truck again, missing me by a half inch. The truck rocked sideways another couple of feet. There was a blast and a simultaneous flash from inside as the shotgun fired and the sound of more breaking glass and things falling down.

I fired the Glock three or four times into the engine block with absolutely no effect. The Hummer had reversed again, and I watched as the wheels quickly cranked and zeroed in on me. I swung the Glock up to the windshield, and fired three quick rounds just as the Hummer leapt forward and then swept past me in a giant explosion.

Dog in the Ram Charger, flames painted across his hood, broadsided the Hummer, knocking it fifteen feet and slamming it into a phone pole.

Everything was silent for a long moment. A couple of pieces of glass tinkled when they fell to the floor from inside the ice cream truck behind me. I walked toward the Hummer, Glock raised, ready to shoot whoever came out. Dog backed up, stumbled out of the Ram Charger and fell down onto his knees, coughing, spitting, and laughing in a sort of insane, crazy way. He had his pistol in his hand. Nothing moved from inside the Hummer as the engine steamed and hissed.

I looked through the smashed passenger window, into the face of a black guy I'd never seen before. He stared back, glassy eyed, mouth open, very dead.

His partner was a red-headed guy with a scraggly beard that made him look like a pedophile. I didn't recognize him either, not that it mattered now. He sat pinned behind the steering wheel with a hole in his forehead about the size of a nickel. There was another hole, just below his right cheek bone. The exit wound had taken off most of his right ear and a fist-sized section of the back of his skull.

I heard something behind me. It was Dog, ripping the back door to the ice cream truck open.

"Don't," he shouted.

I approached the truck cautiously, pistol pointed toward the door where Dog stood. He looked back at me, shook his head, coughed something up and spit into the truck.

"Stupid bastard shot himself," he said, then stepped inside, and opened the top of one of the coolers.

"Jesus," I mumbled.

Baldy was seated on the floor, head tilted back, mouth open, and a disbelieving stare on his face. A gaping wound where his chest had been with the shotgun and the floor around him soaked in blood. The shotgun apparently discharged when the Hummer hit the truck.

"You want some of this ice cream?" Dog sounded nonchalant as he pulled boxes of ice cream treats out of the freezer.

"Come on, we better get the hell out of here, man," I said.

"Yeah, whoa, lookey here," Dog said, pulling two purple bank bags out of the freezer, laying them on top of the boxes of ice cream treats.

They looked just like the bag Baldy had dropped in the bank's night deposit the other evening.

"Dog, come on, we gotta get going. The cops are probably on the way, now."

"Coming," he said, carrying three boxes of ice cream treats and the two purple bank bags over to his truck. He threw them onto the seat between us then jimmied the screwdriver in the ignition until the truck turned over.

"Open up one of them boxes. Give me an ice cream," he said, pulling around the Hummer and heading out to the lake place.

Chapter Fifty-Two

We both heard the siren at the same time. Dog took the next right and quickly pulled over. A police squad raced past behind us, heading in the direction of the ice cream truck and what was left of the Hummer.

"Let's just get out of here," I said.

"Don't need to tell this old Dog twice," he said, then pointed us toward I-35 North and the lake.

By the time we pulled in the engine had a noticeable ping and steam was coming out from beneath the buckled hood.

"Shit, coolant, oil...we might as well have dropped bread crumbs. Any damn idiot could follow our trail from downtown," Dog said, shutting the truck off. The engine clanked, shook, vibrated a bit and then steam hissed from beneath the deep creases in the hood.

"Son-of-a-bitch might blow."

"You kidding?" I asked.

"Naw, just giving you some shit. Come on, you carry the ice cream. I'll take care of the money," he said, climbing out.

Dog slit the nylon bags with the knife he always carried and dumped the contents out onto the plywood counter.

"Holy shit, will you look at this, man?"

I was attempting to cram the ice cream boxes into the frost-filled freezer compartment.

"What the…"

Dog had emptied out the two bags into one large pile of currency. He grabbed two fistfuls of bills.

"There's probably five or six grand here, man! Whew, damn just look at all this shit!"

"Let's count it up," I said, stepping over to the counter.

"You count it, I'm gonna celebrate," he said, opening the refrigerator and pulling out a box of ice cream treats.

I was quickly sorting currency into stacks of hundreds, fifties, and twenties, carefully facing each bill the same way.

"Hey Dev, will you look at this shit here? Jesus Christ."

Dog had taken the top off a box of ice cream treats, only it wasn't full of ice cream. Bundles of currency were neatly wrapped and arranged inside the box. Each bundle labeled with a handwritten '$5000' in blue ballpoint.

"There's fifty grand in this damn thing," he said looking up at me wild eyed. He tossed the box on the counter where I stood, then tore the other two boxes out of the freezer and pulled the cover off the first one.

"Shit, ice cream," he said, dropped the box onto the floor and tore the lid off the second box.

"Shit, more ice cream, damn it. You want one?" he asked, down on his knees, scooping up a handful of treats and stuffing them back into the freezer.

"Let me count this up first," I said, losing count and starting all over again.

When we finished we agreed there was something in the neighborhood of sixty two thousand and change. It took four separate efforts. I never really arrived at the same figure twice, but I was always in the same neighborhood.

"Lot a damn dough for just selling ice cream," I said. I was in the process of finishing my second drumstick, stuffing the tail end of the cone into my mouth.

Dog's lips, beard, and mustache were coated in melted Fudgesicle. He wiped his hands across his T-shirt and began to tear the wrapper off another one.

"You know, that's a lot of goddamn money. You think that little stand was capable of pulling all that in?"

"I don't know. Maybe, I guess. The All Star game is day after tomorrow. That could be some heavy betting action."

"Reason I'm asking is, let's say they didn't do all this action. They're taking bets, but maybe they're also a collection point for other places. Swirlee had more than one truck, right?"

"Yeah, he's got a lot of trucks, or at least the company does," I said as I remembered Swirlee was lying on a block of ice down at the morgue.

"If they were all taking bets, or even some of them, I would guess your girlfriend, Linda, is it?"

"Lola," I said.

"I would guess your girlfriend Lola's got more bad actors on her payroll. You see what I'm getting at?"

I nodded, then said,

"The two guys in the Hummer, I'd never seen either one of them before. So she's got at least two guys we know of still hanging around."

"My guess would be more than two. They come looking for us we could be in real deep shit. And that kind of money is a pretty good reason to come looking," Dog said then crammed half a Fudgesicle into his mouth.

Chapter Fifty-Three

We divided up the money that night. I took thirty and let Dog have the thirty plus, which made him very happy. I also paid back the twenty-five hundred for the Regal and tossed in another five hundred dollars for interest just because I felt generous.

Dog carefully covered his bed with his share of the money, then lay on top of the bills and began snoring. I settled into the recliner and eventually fell asleep with the reloaded Glock lying next to me.

I watched the sunrise news. They mentioned an early morning traffic accident downtown that claimed the lives of three individuals. They ran a five-second shot of the Hummer wrapped against the phone pole, then moved on to a story about the home-run derby scheduled before the All Star Game. A little later I woke Dog up and had him give me a ride to The Spot so I could pick up my car.

"I wasn't sure we were gonna make it," I said as the Ram Charger wheezed into the alley behind my car.

"You're telling me. Sucker's going right into the shop from here." With that I climbed out and watched as he clanged and pinged down the alley and around the corner.

Ten minutes later I was parked and on my cell.

"Yes," Lola answered after about the fifth ring.

"Dev Haskell."

"Yeah, I was waiting for your call. Look, I can't meet you this morning. Something's come up."

"Like what?"

"Oh, just a little staffing problem, is all. Tomorrow morning would work a lot better for me."

"I would really like to get this taken care of." I pushed.

"Believe me, so do I, but I just can't today. Tomorrow?"

"I'll call you," I said, then hung up.

I reclined the seat and waited to see what, if anything, came down the alley to Swirlee's house. I dozed off in the heat and humidity of the afternoon. The car doors slamming from in front of Swirlee's garage woke me. There were two guys. I didn't catch the first one, but the second one wore glasses and had a ponytail with sideburns that followed his jaw line and tapered to a point. He was one of the guys I had expected to see last night.

My phone rang.

"Haskell Investigations," I answered after checking the caller ID.

"Oh, so now you're answering."

"Hi Jill, how are you?"

"Still pretty pissed off, if you want the truth. Where the hell were you?"

"Something came up I had to deal with." I was going to say a staffing problem like Lola had told me, but thought better of the idea.

"You know you still could have phoned."

"Hey, I planned to, but you made it pretty clear not to call, ever, if I remember correctly."

"That was later, but yeah, it might not have been a good idea to call me at that point. Look, I…"

They were back out behind the garage, ponytail, and the dumb looking guy with the crew cut, not running, but not wasting time either. They were driving some sort of red thing. I couldn't tell what it was, but wrote the plate number down on an empty Starbuck's cup as they made a U-turn in the alley, then backed up toward me. The garage door opened and the Mercedes pulled out. Lola sat in the passenger seat, and some ugly guy with sunglasses acted as a chauffer.

"… I mean if you still wanted to. Hello, hello?"

I started the Regal, and waited a moment before I followed.

"Sorry, Jill, I must have hit a dead spot there. I just came out of a tunnel. What were you saying?"

There was a pause while she considered.

"I was saying, do you want to get together sometime? If you don't, just say so. I don't have to be throwing…"

"Jill, Jill, calm down, I would love to get together. I just have some stuff going on right now that requires me to sort of be on call. We can plan something, but I may have to cancel at the last minute. That's all I'm saying."

"Sorry, it's just been an upsetting couple of weeks, you know?"

"Yeah, believe me, I know."

"Look, I'm doing brats on the grill tonight. Just show up. If you can make it, great. If you can't, don't worry. Fair?"

"Yeah. Look, if I can't make it I'll…"

"No, if you can't make it, don't worry. Okay?"

"Okay. And thanks for being patient with me."

I followed Lola and company to the Mr. Swirlee building. Both vehicles drove into the garage. I went up the street, pulled over and then waited.

Lola's Mercedes, complete with chauffer, exited a little after four. It was followed by the two guys in the red car. They drove to the bank and parked in the lot. Lola entered the bank, carrying a couple of purple bags. She returned four or five minutes later. She got back in the passenger side and the Mercedes drove off with the red car following behind.

They stopped at a traffic light and the red car made a right turn while the Mercedes waited for the light to change. I decided to follow the Mercedes. We hadn't traveled more than two blocks when something caught my attention in the rearview mirror. The red car was a block behind me and coming up fast.

Suddenly the Mercedes came to a complete stop in the middle of the street. I was two cars behind. The vehicles ahead of me began to honk, but thought better of it as a rather large man with sunglasses and a Hawaiian print shirt quickly climbed out of the car. His shirt was untucked and his hand had gone into his waistband remaining there while he walked in my direction. He looked very determined. Cars farther back began honking, but stopped when the two thugs jumped out of the red car and began running toward me.

I waited about half a second and then cranked the Regal left across oncoming traffic. A car screeched to a stop, and blared the horn as I shot across the street. I bounced up a small driveway, then turned and raced down the sidewalk in the opposite direction. My two pals from the red car, ponytail and dummy, had crossed the street to head me off, but I shot past and they had to jump out of the way. I tore across the grass boulevard, bounced over the curb and back into the street. I saw the red car making a U-turn in my rearview mirror just as I turned down a side street. I raced down an alley, praying some kid didn't come flying out of a garage or a back yard. At the far end of the alley I caught the red car in my mirror as it streaked past. I could hear the tires screech from a block away and quickly turned left, then took another left into the next alley and raced up to the far end.

I waited for a moment, then zigzagged to a major intersection, and from there onto I-94, figuring they'd never find me in rush-hour bumper-to-bumper. After a half hour of driving aimlessly and checking in my rearview mirror I stopped for provisions, then headed to Jill's.

Chapter Fifty-Four

I arrived carrying four bottles of chilled wine and a thirty-five dollar cake with marzipan frosting from Wuollet's Bakery on Grand Avenue.

"Wow, what, did you win the lottery or something? You didn't have to do this, Dev."

She was wearing white shorts and the 'T' from her blue thong was riding maybe a half inch above the back of her waistband. She had on a strappy top that was cut off, exposing a flat stomach and almost, but not quite, her boobs. Not for lack of trying to look on my part.

"Throw that wine in the fridge, will you? Give me that cake. How did you know?" she asked, opening up the white bakery box.

"I just thought...well you know as a peace offering. I..."

"Stop groveling, okay? Pour me a glass of wine and if you want beer you know where it is."

Over brats, beer, and wine we fenced back and forth verbally. I refilled her wine glass, not for the first time, brought both of us a large piece of cake, then asked,

"Can we go over some Mr. Swirlee stuff?"

"Why do you care about that jerk? He's dead and the world is a much better place," she said, then took another forkful of cake.

"Yeah, I know, just trying to figure out the operation. Did you know he was running a betting shop out of some of his trucks?"

She looked at me like I was nuts, took a healthy swallow of wine and seemed to compose herself.

"This is news? Years back he was involved with the rackets as they called it. Gambling, prostitution, I've even heard drugs. Mind you I don't have any proof. To my knowledge he was never caught. To be honest, he was never even investigated as far as I know."

"You know anything about his girlfriend, this Lola woman? I think her real name is Lucille something."

"Lentz. Yes, Lucille Lentz and no, I don't know much about her anymore. Well, except I don't think she's just his girlfriend, she's his niece as well, to tell you the truth."

"His niece?"

"That's what I heard."

"What do you mean, you don't know much about her anymore?"

"Just that I sort of knew her as a kid, a very young kid. We played together, you know? I really haven't seen her for years."

"So did you know Swirlee, too? You said your grandfather..."

"Yeah, sure, a quarter of a century ago. Look, what do you care? He ended up the way of all bad guys...dead. Say, you're cool with the police now on that whole thing, aren't you?"

"Who, me? Yeah, all cleared up," I lied. "I just sort of wondered about the guy is all."

She eyed me for a moment, then drained her glass and held it out toward me. About three and a half bottles later we were stumbling up the steps and into her bed. We wrestled as only drunken lovers can, then passed out. Later that night as she snored in bed next to me, I lay awake and tried to answer the question Jill had asked. Why did I care?

Chapter Fifty-Five

I got back to Dog's around noon. As soon as his shack came into sight I stopped. A dark blue Crown Victoria was parked in front of the screen door. I quietly backed away, then got out and approached the shack through the mud in the back. I crept up to the shack and peeked in through a grimy window. Dog was sitting in the recliner, sipping a beer and watching a black-and-white movie, alone.

"What the hell do you think you're doing?" I asked a few moments later, tracking mud and weeds into the kitchen.

He laughed, then said,

"I heard ya drive up, watched you back out, figured that Crown Vic would get you. It's the loaner from the body shop."

"Thing looks like a cop car," I said.

"Don't it? You find anything else out about your girlfriend?"

"Yeah, she'll do anything, but she really likes…"

"I meant Swirlee's chick."

"You mean Lola? Well, she said she had a staffing problem yesterday and couldn't meet. I was following them later in the day, but they spotted me, or at least the car. Chased me a little. Don't know if they actually recognized me or just my car tailing them."

"How many?"

"Guys? Three of them. Two I recognized. One, a big guy I've never seen before. I'd say after the other night it would appear they've tightened things up. You called the cops, right?"

"Yeah, thought I told ya. They took my information. You know how they get. You never really know what they're thinking. I mean, I gave them the license numbers and later that night one of the vehicles is all smashed up with two dead bastards in it. You'd think that might ring some bells, but then again..."

"I gotta get to Lola, keep pressure on her," I said, taking my phone out and calling.

Dog lowered the sound with his remote.

She answered on the second ring

"Lola, please."

"Dev, is that you?" She actually sounded nice.

"Hi, Lola. Yeah, it's me. Hey, what are the chances of us getting together this afternoon?"

"I can do that. Listen, why don't you come over for a late lunch? Maybe some special afternoon delight. I've been kind of starved for company..."

"No, that won't work. I got a better idea. You know City Hall?"

"City Hall?"

"Meet me at the base of the Indian statue, Vision of Peace or whatever it's called. Probably be best if you come alone."

"A little dramatic, don't you think?"

"Just trying to be careful. See you at three?"

"I'll be there."

"City Hall? The courthouse? Are you nuts?" Dog shouted when I hung up.

214

"Think about it…a very public place, cops all around…you have to go through metal detectors to get in there. It's perfect for us."

"Us?"

"I'll need you hanging somewhere in the background, just to keep me safe."

"What are you gonna tell her?"

"I'm still fine-tuning that part of the deal." Actually I had no idea.

Chapter Fifty-Six

We got to City Hall an hour early, then hung around by the elevators on the lower level. We blended with the crowd, looking like two more low-life's just waiting for our case to be called. At ten minutes before three I said to Dog,

"I'm going up to the main floor. Wait here about five minutes, then come on up. Just act like you're waiting for a lawyer or something. Don't crowd me."

"I gotta tell you, man, this place gives me the creeps. Nothing good has ever happened to me here. My first sentence was handed down in this building. I was fifteen. I've never really liked the place since."

"Just relax, what can go wrong? Like I said, they got cops and metal detectors up there watching everything coming in. We're safe."

I took the elevator up to the ground floor, got out and walked toward the base of the statue. At almost forty feet high and made of polished onyx it wouldn't be easy to miss. I passed a painter dressed in white pants and T-shirt setting up. There were maybe a half dozen unhappy people drifting around and all looking like they were waiting for someone. They all wore a similar sort of stressed look. Like Dog said, nothing

216

good ever happened to him in this building. By the looks on all the faces that still seemed to be the case.

"Dev?"

It was Lola, and almost ten minutes ahead of schedule.

"Lola, hey, you're early. Wow, I didn't think women did that sort of thing," I said, stalling for time, hoping Dog would magically appear.

"Come on, let's go," she said, grabbing me by the arm.

"No, I like it right here," I said, planting my feet.

"I don't think so," she said, then nodded behind her. The painter in white stepped forward. Unfortunately, he suddenly looked a lot like the guy in the Hawaiian-print shirt from yesterday.

"Don't be an asshole," he said, then shoved a small revolver into my back.

"We're going right out the door," Lola said, tugging on my arm again. "Just one big happy family. Before you get any ideas, take a good look at the security guard there...three hundred pounds of blubber who doesn't want to be involved with any trouble you bring his way. So do us all a favor and just walk out quietly."

We headed toward the door. It suddenly became obvious to me you only passed through security when you entered. I was being led out at gunpoint and no one was going to know.

We walked past the line formed to enter the metal detector. Past the three hundred pound guard who looked bored out of his mind. Lola seemed to snuggle against me, grabbing my arm even tighter. She smiled at the guard, then said to me, "You did very well in there, very well. I'm so proud of you."

"They got a gun here," I said loudly and attempted to pull away. A couple of people in line glanced over at us, bored. Lola clasped my arm tighter, smiling. The painter punched the revolver into my kidney.

"Sorry, we've had a commitment hearing," she said to the guard by way of explanation and kept walking.

He paused thinking for just a nanosecond before he nodded knowingly. People ranting in here were an everyday occurrence. He couldn't have cared less and went back to placing the next briefcase on a conveyor to be scanned.

The three of us stepped into the revolving door, the painter with his gun right behind me.

"That was really stupid. Shoot his balls off if he does anything else," Lola said.

We exited the revolving door. The dumb-looking guy and his pal with the ponytail fell in on either side of us.

"Any problems?"

"Nothing we can't take care of. He tries anything, you two hold him. I told Benton to shoot his balls off." She let go of my arm and slid the side door open on a van waiting at the curb.

"Get your ass in there," Benton the painter said from behind me, then jammed the gun into my kidney again.

218

Chapter Fifty-Seven

No one said anything during the drive. I had
Benton squeezed in next to me holding a revolver. The
dopey guy with the crew cut sat behind me, holding a
weapon. The jerk with the ponytail sat in the front
passenger seat and pointed a very large automatic at
me while Lola drove.

"I don't think we've been introduced," I said,
looking around.

Benton clicked the hammer on his small revolver,

"I can put a couple of these in you. They'll rattle
around and rip you up inside, or you can just shut up.
Your choice."

I nodded.

Fifteen minutes later the garage door at the Mr.
Swirlee building opened. Lola drove in and parked in
front of a loading dock. The Mercedes and the red car,
a Ford of some sort, were backed into two spaces
against a far wall.

Benton slid the door open, stepped out, but never
took his eyes or the revolver off me.

"Get your ass out here, funny man."

Lola was already up on the loading dock, purse
over her shoulder, clicking her high heels into a

darkened office area. The other two goons remained focused on me.

I climbed out of the van, kept my hands halfway raised and followed the wave of Benton's revolver as it directed me up the small loading-dock stairs.

"Stop, right there," Benton said when I'd taken two or three steps across the dock.

He hurried up the stairs, walked in front of me, and looked in the office. Before I knew what happened he'd spun around and kicked me on the chin. I went down, rolled to the side, started to get up when I felt a blast to my nose, then a second or two of weightlessness before I landed on the cold concrete next to the van.

"Guess you can't fly none too well." Dopey chuckled.

"Quit screwing around and bring him in here," Lola called from the office.

I coughed up blood and spit it onto the floor as I got up on all fours. Things were blurry and I could tell blood was flowing freely from my nose. Hands grabbed me from either side and half dragged me toward the stairs. I was having trouble walking.

"Goddamn it, I told you I wanted to ask him some questions. I won't get any answers if he's dead, now will I?" Lola screamed.

"He fell off the dock. We thought he was trying to get away."

I couldn't tell who was talking.

"Get him cleaned up. And don't let him bleed all over everything. Jesus, I got staff back in tomorrow morning. I don't need any more problems right now. Get him a towel or something." She waited a second or two then shrieked, "Come on, damn it, move."

A few minutes later I held a wet towel over my nose. When I tried to close my bottom jaw it felt like the alignment was off by about a half inch. The wet towel felt good, but it smelled like gasoline or motor oil.

"Sorry about that. Feeling better, Dev?" Lola asked soothingly. If I didn't know better I would have thought she really cared.

I pulled the towel away. I could detect the broken bridge of my nose swelling, blocking part of my vision. My nose was plugged and I had to breathe out of my mouth.

"Hell of a way to get me on your side," I said, then felt the blood streaming from my nose again.

Lola shot a look at Benton, who just smiled and shrugged his shoulders.

"Put your head back, Dev. Just relax. Now, I've got a problem. Actually, I've got close to a hundred thousand problems. But I'm pretty sure you can fix all that for me."

I took the towel away from my face.

"No, believe me, you're not that much fun to look at right now. Lean back, that's right, put the towel back up there. See, as much as some of us would like to kill you, we're not going to do that. Are we?"

I didn't hear any agreement.

"Anyway, you're such a top notch P.I. and all...I want you to find out who stole a hundred grand from me the other night. Who's trying to shut down my operation? I don't know how, but find out. I'll give you forty-eight hours."

I felt like telling her it wasn't a hundred grand, it was only sixty and some change, but figured it might make more sense to just shut up.

"Now, if you don't find out…well, you remember that guy who tried to fly out the window the other day, don't you?"

Pinky Ackerman, I thought, but didn't let on I knew.

"We already checked. He can't fly." One of the thugs laughed behind me.

Lola looked past me disapprovingly, then said, "Oh, and if you have any thoughts about doing your usual something stupid, you know, like going to the police, here's a little added incentive." She nodded at Benton who stepped into a dark office and rolled out a desk chair.

The chair was grey, with armrests, and squeaked slightly. Jill's arms and feet were taped to the chair. Her jeans were torn and bloodied on both knees. There were two dark bruises on her arms. She had duct tape covering her mouth. Benton grabbed her by the hair and pulled her head back. One of her eyes was blackened, swollen almost closed, the other looked scared to death.

"Just remember, you don't come across and your little lover is liable to end up in bed with your new friends here. And when they're done, I'll feed her to my dogs. I promise," Lola said.

Benton smiled at me then bent over and ran his tongue up the side of Jill's face.

"She's gonna be a lot of fun." He laughed.

"Now, get him the hell out of my sight. Take him back to City Hall, where he feels safe," Lola snarled.

Benton drove the van while the other two kept their guns on me. They stopped a block away from City Hall, and the guy behind me slid the side door open. As I got out, he said, "Hey, Haskell. She ain't kidding. We'd love to have a go at that girlfriend of

222

yours." Then he made a licking motion with his tongue and they drove off laughing.

Chapter Fifty-Eight

People walking past were giving me a wide berth. I still felt groggy and held the blood-soaked towel against my nose. Blood was splattered down my shirt and onto my jeans. I phoned Dog.

"Where the hell are you, man? I've been looking all over for you," he said.

"Things didn't quite go according to plan. Can you come and get me?"

"You sound like shit. You okay?"

"Just come and get me," I said, then told him where I was.

"Jesus, you're gonna need a doctor," Dog said ten minutes later when I climbed into the Crown Victoria.

"Just get me home."

We were three and a half hours in emergency. I walked out with a nose splint, pain pills, and a splitting headache.

On the way home Dog said, "Look, don't be pissed off at me, Dev. But I've been here before. You feel like shit now, but you'd feel even worse tomorrow if you didn't get that splint and those pills. You're gonna just have to take it easy for a couple of days."

"There's no time to take it easy. I gotta get a hundred grand to them," I groaned.

"A hundred grand? Where'd that come from?"

"I guess from the other night, with the truck and Hummer and all."

"First of all it wasn't no hundred grand. Second of all, we found it, free and clear. Not like we went looking to score. It just sort of happened. Finders keepers, man. I told you we should have taken those guys…"

"They got Jill."

"Jill?"

"Yeah, they got her. Unless I get the money to them they're…"

"The money? Jesus, are you ready to stop playing around with these fucks and deal with the problem? It's obvious they don't take you as much of a threat. Certainly nothing to worry about. They know about me?"

"No, at least I don't think so. I never mentioned anything."

"They're about to find out, man."

"Look, can we just go home? It's been kind of a horseshit day, ya know? I gotta figure out what I'm gonna do."

"Here's the deal, Dev. They won't do anything to her until you get the money to them. But, once they got the money, there's nothing to stop them from killing both of you."

Unfortunately I couldn't argue with his logic.

Chapter Fifty-Nine

If two pain pills made me groggy, six knocked
me out.

"Fuck, it's already after ten," I said, jumping out
of the recliner the next morning.

"Told you those pills would work," Dog said,
sipping a mug of coffee.

"I gotta get that money to them, or else…"

"Or else nothing. Look I been thinking, man, and
you got a couple of things in your favor…maybe,
sorta. But one thing that won't help is giving them a
hundred grand. That gets you nowhere. If they're that
hot for the money, they're feeling pressure. I'm
guessing they have to cover bets on that All Star game.
So we can use that to our advantage."

"Dog, they're going to kill her."

"No, they're not. At least not yet, so stay cool."

"I should call Aaron. He'll…"

"Your cop pal? Look, I'm sure he'd help, but
they're gonna lock you up first and then sort it out.
That'll take a week. We got a little time, but we ain't
got a week, pal."

"So, what do I do?"

"First thing, we need to go to the bank."

__Chapter Sixty__

"See, this is exactly the reason I don't like to tidy up the place. Where would we be if you'd tossed all this shit out?" Dog asked as he opened a beer, then went back to digging through a trash bag.

We were back from the bank, with three grand in cash, two grand in hundreds, the rest ones. Dog had me sorting the cash, wrapping the old bands with the handwritten $5000 in blue ballpoint around the bundles. I placed a hundred dollar bill on the top and bottom of each stack with the ones stuffed in the middle.

"Don't you think they're gonna fan through these things, see all ones?"

"No." He took another sip of beer.

"You want to maybe give that a little more thought?"

"No. I already have. Look, they'll be nervous, waiting for you to maybe try something. They need the cash. All they're gonna see is hundreds, and not think beyond that. Plus, they'll be planning to take you and the chick out…"

"Her name is Jill."

"…soon as you deliver this dough."

"You're sure?"

"No." He sipped. "But you start trying to play every option and you'll drive yourself nuts."

"Jesus, I don't know if this is gonna work," I said, looking at the stacks of cash.

"Course it will, relax. Stuff those in here," Dog said, fishing an ice cream box out of the trash bag and tossing it on the counter.

I arranged the dummy stacks of hundreds in the box.

"I gotta admit," I said. "At least it looks like the stuff we grabbed. But now what?"

"Call 'em and ask for more time."

"More time?"

"They won't give it to you, but if you were working this you wouldn't have figured out what happened yet, would you? Hell, the news reported it as a car accident. If the cops knew we were involved, don't you think you would have heard something? A phone call from your pal Alan or…"

"Aaron."

"Yeah, whatever."

"Call that broad, ask her for more time. She's gonna tell you no, but it'll help convince her you're actually trying to do something."

As frightening as it sounded, I couldn't argue with Dog's logic.

"Hi, Lola. Dev Haskell."

"How's the nose?"

It was swollen, hurt like hell, throbbed nonstop, I couldn't breathe out of it and if I wore the splint it hurt even more.

"It's fine."

"What have you got for me, lover boy?"

"I want to know Jill's all right, first off."

228

"She's sleeping."

"Wake her."

"Don't you want to know with who?"

I was silent for a long moment.

"Ha, ha, ha…touchy, are we? I bet my old girlfriend is pretty good in the love department."

"She had better be okay. If you so much as…"

"Save it, hero. She's fine. For now. What have you got for me?"

"Well, from what I can learn that wasn't a simple car accident the other night with that Hummer and your truck. Turns out…"

"Goddamn it, I don't need a traffic report. I could have told you that yesterday. That's all you have so far? I thought you were supposed to be some hot shot investigator?"

"It takes time, Lola. Look, I'm going to need a couple more days to find out what happened. There aren't a lot of leads here for starters, and the cops aren't talking. By the way, your uncle or whatever Swirlee was…his body in the trunk of my car doesn't make it any easier for me to get police cooperation."

"Then you had better figure something out and fast or plan on taking out a loan. I don't see that cash here, your girlfriend is going to get one hell of a last night to remember. Got it?"

"I just need more time. Why is that so …"

"No," she screamed and hung up.

"Sounded like that went pretty well. You want a beer?" Dog asked, opening the cooler.

Chapter Sixty-One

Cleaning and reassembling my Glock a half dozen times did nothing to calm my nerves.

"Jesus, you're even driving me nuts," Dog complained.

"I feel like I should be doing something."

"You are doing something, Dev. You're putting pressure on. If you're going nuts, just think how crazy things probably are over at the Swirlee household right now."

"Small consolation. God I hope Jill is okay."

"Come on, let's take a look." He set his empty bottle next to the others on the counter.

"Take a look?"

"Yeah, Swirlee's. Not gonna hurt anything to just cruise by. What? You think they're looking out the window, waiting for you? Besides I need to check the joint out."

"What do you expect to find?"

"Find? Nothing. But while you're going in the front door tomorrow night, I'll be in the back. Be nice to have a rough idea of what I'll be dealing with."

"Hey, Dog, I don't know if I've said thanks, but I can't thank you enough for your help. You've been great."

"Just remember, we're even when this deal's over."

"Believe me, if we never mentioned any of this again that would be okay with me. But really, I mean it, thanks."

We went to some burger bar named Charlie's that Dog knew, and oddly, I'd never heard of.

"Place was called Ted's for about a thousand years. Then a guy named Charlie bought it. I don't know that he changed the menu, but at least they wash their hands now before they cook the burgers."

There was a couple shooting pool at a table about six feet away. I caught the woman staring at me a couple of different times. I guessed it was my nose. Eventually, she said something to the guy she was with, he looked over at us a moment, then shook his head. She rubbed his arm a few times and suddenly they were out the door and never finished their game.

Dog caught it, looked at me, and said, "She must know you."

"Look, I know I've said this before, but, well, shouldn't we be doing something?" I dragged my last French fry through a ketchup slick.

"We are doing something. You want another?" he asked, signaling the bartender with his empty glass.

I shook my head no.

"We're waitin' till dark, then I'm gonna recon the place, maybe get a little head start. You're gonna phone what's-her-face…"

"Lola."

"Tomorrow morning, you beg for more time, then agree to be there with the cash at ten tomorrow night."

"Why ten?"

"You know, sometimes I wonder if there's anyone home up there. 'Cause the All Star game is tomorrow night, out on the West Coast. Ring any bells? They're two hours behind us. Things will just be getting under way, and Swirlee's little pal will be feeling the pressure."

Dog lingered over his beer for fifteen minutes, a long linger for him.

"Come on, let's get going. You drive," he said, tossing me the keys. "I want to get a good look as we go past."

It was dark as we drove down Summit Avenue, past Swirlee's house.

"Jesus, and only one dude lives in that place? Joint is huge, man. Keep going a couple of blocks then take a left and park," Dog instructed.

When I pulled over he said, "Pop the trunk. You just sit here until I'm back. Okay?"

I nodded.

He closed the trunk, and walked around to my window, carrying a trash bag.

"I shouldn't be more than thirty minutes. Stay put, got it?"

"What's in the …"

His glare cut me off.

"Okay, I'll be here."

He returned about forty-five minutes later.

"I'll tell you this…they got the joint more or less buttoned up."

"Those damn dogs out?"

"Things work right, I don't think they'll be much of a problem," he said, then looked over at me and smiled.

"If you shot those dogs Lola's likely to snap. She'll hurt Jill, maybe even kill her."

"Relax, I just brought the puppies a little treat."

"What was in the trash bag? You didn't poison those things, did you?"

"Not to worry. They'll be fine, just out of the way for the next thirty-six hours or so."

"What was in the trash bag?"

"A raccoon I shot earlier, mixed with some shit Noleen left behind."

I shot a glance in his direction.

"Relax, they'll just be a little psychotic for twenty-four hours. Look, by the time they get it all analyzed, if they even bother, we're out of there or dead. Either way it don't much matter now, does it?"

I guessed it didn't.

Chapter Sixty-Two

Dog was still asleep when I phoned Lola the following morning.

"What?" she answered.

"Lola, Dev Haskell, I…"

"I can see that. I'm expecting a call back from my vet, so make it fast."

"Look, I'm coming up with a couple of things but I need a little more time. Can't you just…"

"No, damn it. Were you even listening yesterday? I'm…I mean, you're out of time, do you hear? Now have that money here tonight or you can just forget about your little bedtime friend, got it?"

"Okay, okay. But I want to know she's safe, and I'll want to see her tonight, before I give you anything. Is that clear?"

"You just be sure… oh, here's my other call. Bye," she screamed and hung up.

"That your sweetheart?" Dog called from the bathroom.

"Yeah, and none too sweet."

"Good, that just tells us she's feeling the pressure."

"God, I wish this shit was over," I said.

"It will be," he said, then I heard the toilet flush and he walked into the kitchen scratching himself.

"By the way, you sound a hell of a lot better, like that nose is beginning to heal up," he said.

I suddenly realized I was able to breathe through my nose again.

The day crawled by at a snail's pace, until eventually around eight that night Dog came out of his room, carrying a pile of tan padding.

"Here, man, slip this shit on."

"What the hell is this?"

"A vest. What's it look like?"

"A vest?"

"MTV's," he said. "You know, bullet-proof vest. Put it on, then put your shirt on over it."

"They'll see it, for Christ sake."

"Let's hope so. They're also gonna see the pistol you're carrying. I want the bastards paying attention to you, not looking closely at the cash, and not looking around for me."

"They aren't going to let me in the door carrying a gun. I was planning to exchange the cash for Jill in the open, out in the front yard."

"They ain't gonna let you in for long. I'll take care of that. Look, if it was you, wouldn't you worry if some guy rang your doorbell with a box of cash and just expected to get his girlfriend back? Who in the hell is that stupid?"

Me for one, I guessed, then nodded. "I see your point, sort of."

"Trust me, the good-guy shit don't work. Look, you're gonna be there at ten. Call that bitch and tell her you want to see your darling in the window as you drive by so you know she's at least in the place."

"What if they say no?"

"They won't."

I phoned Lola. She answered on the first ring.

"Are you on your way?"

"I'll be there by ten o'clock, I…"

"You'll have the money, right?"

"Yeah, I should have it. I want to make sure Jill is there and she's okay."

"She will be, as long as you bring the money."

"I'm going to call you around ten. I want to see her in the window when I pull up. If I don't see her, the deal is off."

"And if she's not here?"

"Like I said, no deal. She better be there and she better not be harmed."

"Listen, you just make damn sure…"

This time it was my turn to hang up.

Chapter Sixty-Three

I dropped Dog off a couple blocks away, then waited ten minutes before I pulled in front and phoned.

Lola answered on the first ring.

"Haskell?"

"I'm in front. Let me see Jill."

"You have my money?"

"I want to see Jill."

She mumbled something, and suddenly a light went on in an upstairs room. Jill was at the window. One of the thugs stood next to her.

"There, see her?" Lola asked.

"Have her wave."

Another mumble and Jill gave a tentative wave just before the light went out.

"There, satisfied? Now get the hell in here."

Just as I approached the front gate, there was a buzz, and then the audible click unlocking the thing. I stepped inside the yard. I held the Glock out on top of the ice cream box. I planned to shoot the dogs if I even saw them. The front door opened as I approached and Benton stood in the darkened doorway. I could just make out the stupid grin on his face.

"Lose the gun right there."

I stopped.

"I don't have a snowball's chance in hell if I drop this gun. I got your money here, a hundred grand." I held up the open box.

"Don't look like no hundred grand to me."

"It's all hundreds, dumb shit. Twenty packets, five grand each. You any good at math or just blindsiding people?"

"All hundreds! We didn't have all hundreds. We…"

"You said a hundred grand. That's what I got here, a hundred grand. No one told me it had to be the exact same bills, asshole."

Benton paused, trying to think, maybe.

"It still don't look…"

"Benton, shut up. We don't have time. Haskell, bring that in here. Hold onto your gun if it makes you feel any better," Lola's voice called out from somewhere inside the darkened entry.

I moved forward cautiously, waved Benton back from the doorway with the Glock and then stepped inside.

"Just set it down on the floor," Lola commanded. She was maybe ten feet behind Benton. I didn't see the other two thugs.

"Where's Jill? That was the deal."

"Bring her out," Lola yelled.

Jill suddenly appeared from a room far down the hallway. The thug with the ponytail stood behind and pushed her forward with a hand on her shoulder. Her mouth was still taped, but her hands and feet appeared to be free. The swelling appeared to have gone down on her eye, but even in the dim hall it still looked awfully bruised.

"Take the tape off her mouth," I said.

238

"Go ahead," Lola said as they came up alongside her.

Jill gave a quick shriek when Benton pulled the piece of tape off her mouth and dropped it to the floor.

"Okay, here's your money," I said, setting the box on the floor. "We're gonna just back out and leave." I had the gun pointed in Lola's direction and motioned Jill over toward me.

She glanced at Lola then quickly crossed over to me.

I felt a sudden breeze through the hallway, barely noticeable. The lace curtain on the entry window fluttered ever so slightly.

Benton began to reach for the box.

"Don't," I said, pointing the Glock at his head.

I motioned to Jill, and she quickly went out the door.

"You keep your ass right there. I wanna count this shit," Benton said, reaching for the box.

"Can you count that high?"

He glared at me, then began running his fingers across the stacks, counting them. He pulled two stacks out quickly from the middle of the box, checked the hundred dollar bills.

"This ain't the same money as before."

"I already told you. It's a hundred grand. What the hell do you care as long as it's cash?"

"Yeah, I get that, but see…if it ain't the same money that was stolen from us, how come it's got our bands around it? That's your writing on 'em, see?" He turned for half a second to show Lola.

"Up, up, hands up, now," I shouted.

Benton froze.

"Do like he said," Dog stepped into the hallway, behind Lola and Ponytail.

"Guns on the ground, assholes."

Benton glared at me, but followed my command and placed his gun on the floor.

"You two, drop the guns," Dog said, slowly, loudly.

Ponytail tossed his weapon. It half bounced across the oak floor, then skidded to a stop against the radiator.

"You," Dog said to Lola.

"I just have this cell phone." She raised her hand with the phone.

"That'll do," Dog said taking the phone.

"All of you on the floor. Now. Come on, move," Dog yelled.

He punched in three numbers on the phone, waited a brief moment, then said, "Yeah, nine-one-one, concerned citizen here. I'd like to report shots fired at …" Dog gave the address, then ended the call.

Lola looked from Ponytail to Benton then back at me.

Dog said to Benton lying on the floor,

"You, big guy, you do that kick the other day with your left or right foot?"

Benton just glared.

"You ever play ball?" Dog asked, sounding more casual as he kicked Benton's pistol toward the front door.

"A little," Benton glared up not sure where this was going.

"A little…well not anymore, fuckwit," Dog said, then casually pulled the trigger and shot Benton in the back of his right knee.

I jumped at the sound.

"Oh, Jesus," Ponytail screamed and began to cry.

"You two down on the floor," Dog commanded.

240

"Shit," Benton screamed, then seemed to swallow down the pain and gave a guttural groan.

"Lady, you got a bit of a mess to clean up here and the cops are on the way. Oh, yeah, before I forget…kind of a little problem out in the back. Looks like someone might have had an accident on your patio. Better get that taken care of," he said, then laid the cell phone on her back.

I picked up the guns. Dog grabbed the box of cash and we backed out, closing the door as we left.

"You really call nine-one-one?" I asked, then heard a faint siren in the distance.

"That answer your question?" Dog said.

Chapter Sixty-Four

I drove. Jill was in the passenger seat. Dog was in the backseat. We made it back to the lake place in twenty minutes. On the way Jill told us how they had teased her about stuffing Swirlee's body in the trunk of my car.

"Look, you two need to go down and turn yourself into the police," Dog said. "Call your buddy, what's his name?"

"Aaron LaZelle."

"Yeah, have him waiting for you, or better yet meet him somewhere so he can bring you in. Make your statements. With Jill's tale, they'll have you bonded and out in no time."

"What about you?"

"Me? I'm not turning myself in. They're looking for me on something completely unrelated to tonight. Don't sweat it. You think the cops are gonna believe the bad guys about someone stealing their dough? Not likely. Besides, she's your ticket." He nodded at Jill.

"If I'm the ticket, I need a very hot shower before I do anything else," Jill said.

It was a little after one when I phoned Aaron.

"Yeah, yes," he half groaned himself awake.

"Aaron, Dev."

"Dev, where he hell are you?" He was suddenly wide awake.

"Look, I want to come in, but I'm gonna need your help. I want to make a statement. There's been another incident tonight. I want to clear this shit up. Maybe you can give Manning a ring and have him meet us, if you'll help."

"You know I will. Just tell me where."

Aaron met us downtown, in front of Mickey's Diner about an hour later. He was waiting when Dog dropped us off a block away.

"You two okay?" Aaron said looking at my nose, then glancing at Jill's eye.

"Yeah, the bad news is, the nose is actually on the mend. Aaron, this is Jill. She's a client of mine. She was kidnapped two days ago by Lola Lentz and held against her will. She'll be able to provide information on Mr. Swirlee's murder, Bernie Sneen's murder, and a couple of other things that are hanging fire for you guys."

"Lieutenant LaZelle," Aaron said, going official and extending his hand to Jill. "Dev, you know you're likely to be held, but let's start getting this straightened out. Goddamn it, I've been worried about you. I don't know if I should hug you or strangle you. Come on."

Manning was waiting for us in the lobby. I'll give him this much, he was a professional. But no one has the right to be looking that positive and chipper in the wee hours of the morning.

I waived my right to an attorney. Jill was at my side. Aaron stayed with me. Neither one of us mentioned Dog. By the end of things I was sputtering along on no sleep and too much bad coffee.

"And did they tell you when they placed the body in the trunk of Mr. Haskell's car?" Manning asked Jill for about the sixth or seventh time. We sat in the same interview room I'd been in before. The Formica table with the cigarette burns between us.

"Like I told you earlier, they just said it was late, then made that joke about standing in front of the open trunk as some guys walked down the street because the bar had closed. That would make it after one, right?"

Manning gave a noncommittal nod.

"And then what?" he asked.

"Then they joked about stealing Dev's golf clubs. You know, so the body would fit into the car. They thought it was funny. One of them said it would probably improve his game."

"And you can identify this bag?" he asked me.

"Black bag, white side pockets, red letters on the bag spelling out *Taylor Made* on either side. An opened twelve pack of Titleist balls, three maybe four balls in there. Plus a flask with some Jameson. Oh, and a black bra," I said this last bit under my breath.

"Pardon me, what was that?" Manning asked. He was writing things down as I spoke.

"A black bra," I said, speaking a little louder.

"Yeah, that's what I thought," Manning said.

Jill shook her head disgustedly.

They drove Jill home, but continued to grill me, although the intensity had let up considerably.

Eventually Manning said, "Mr. Haskell, I'm going to send you home. I would like to point out that none of this had to be this hard. If you had cooperated with us to begin with a lot of the aggravation you've had, and certainly Miss Lydell has had to deal with, could have been avoided. While you were successful in freeing her from being held, that could have really backfired. I still have some questions on that, but they'll keep. I'd like to see what our people on the scene come up with."

I nodded. It sounded as though things might be breaking my way for a change.

"In the meantime, I don't think it's too much to ask that you check in with us, daily. That sound acceptable to you, Mr. Haskell?"

Another one of those police questions that really weren't questions.

"I'd be happy to do that, Detective."

That got me a flashed smile, and in no time I was on my way home in the rear of a squad car.

There was a chalk circle around the stain in my driveway where my car used to sit. My Buick Regal was still out at Dog's lake place and I thought it might be best if it just stayed there for a while. I needed a hot shower and bed.

Chapter Sixty-Five

I slept until the following morning. I'm sure being in a bed as opposed to a recliner and not listening to Dog's snoring had nothing to do with it.

I phoned Jill after a lunch of BLT and a couple of Leinenkugel beers.

"Hey Jill."

"Oh, hi."

"Get a good night's sleep?"

"Yeah."

"How's the eye?"

"Fine."

"How are you feeling?"

"Fine."

"Mmm-mmm. Look, I was wondering if you wanted to get together maybe later today?"

"No."

"Okay. It sounds like you might have some other things going on."

"Whatever."

"Yeah, look I'll call you in a couple of days. Hopefully we…"

She hung up.

There you had it, a black eye, a kidnapping, threatened rape, throw in a little kneecapping and suddenly I'm not the fun date I used to be. Go figure.

I phoned Heidi later that afternoon.

"Hey, Heidi."

"Hi."

"Just checking in. How are things?"

"Fine."

"Just wondered if you wanted to get together later tonight, I don't know, maybe have dinner, couple of drinks." I didn't want to push and suggest we end up in her bed.

"No, I don't think so."

"I see…well, look, I'll give you a call later. Maybe…"

Heidi hung up.

I phoned Karen. I'd been thinking of her ever since I mentioned her bra in my golf bag to Detective Manning. I decided not to mention the possibility of the police calling about her missing underwear.

"Hey, Karen, Dev Haskell."

"I told you never to call me," she said, then hung up.

It was dark, sometime after nine thirty. I'd finished my liquid dinner of Leinenkugel beers chased down by a couple of Jamesons. I was sitting at my kitchen counter, well into my dessert course, a heavy helping of pity chased down by another Jameson. There was a knock on my back door.

When I peeked out the hair style didn't look familiar. Her back was turned to me, as if she were checking out the yard. Who cared? Tight jeans on a great ass…her timing was perfect, so I opened the door.

"Hi, there, what…"

Ponytail's shotgun was up under my chin, backing me into the room.

Lola followed.

"Should've known you'd live in some sort of dump like this. I want my money," she screamed.

"Gee." I half giggled. "If I had your money, do you think I'd be in a dump like…"

She nodded to Ponytail who slammed the butt of the shotgun into my stomach, hard. I doubled over and fought to keep all the Jameson down.

"I don't think you quite understand where I'm coming from, Mr. Haskell."

Then she picked up my whiskey glass and threw it against the door frame. Waterford makes a very distinctive sound when it breaks.

"Believe me, I'd like nothing more than to castrate you with a dull knife, then shoot you a half dozen times. But, even though that would make me feel a lot better, it wouldn't really help, would it?" she said looking around.

"No, that would definitely not…"

"Shut up. What the hell is that wretched thing?" she asked looking at my Muskie hanging on the wall.

Ponytail grabbed the collar of my shirt and yanked me to my feet.

I had to swallow my stomach down again.

"That? That's my prize Muskie."

"Not anymore," she said pulled a knife out of the rack and sliced off its head in one quick swoop. The head bounced on the counter then shot off at an angle and spun around on the floor by the backdoor.

"I take it you don't fancy sea food," I said.

Ponytail didn't have to be told. He just slammed the shotgun into me again, hard, knocking me down.

"Listen, smartass. I want that money. Fast. You don't deliver, and I'm gonna kill your little girlfriend and then I'm gonna kill you. Maybe not tomorrow, but I will. You can't protect her forever. And I had better not see that maniac friend of yours or any cops. If I do, the girlfriend is dead. Understand?"

I looked up, and nodded yes, fighting to keep my stomach down.

She stormed into the night. Ponytail backed out behind her, stopped long enough to kick the Muskie head at me, then slammed the door.

Chapter Sixty-Six

"The answer's the same one as before. We gotta take them out," Dog said.

We were driving back to the lake place. Dog had picked me up as soon as I called.

"Oh, and who can blame her for not wanting to hear from you, but you better call Jill and tell her to disappear until this is taken care of. This Swirlee bitch isn't screwing around."

"Damn it, I really thought I was done with this."

Dog shook his head, but didn't say anything.

We attempted to brainstorm, but didn't really come up with any new ideas, other than we needed a break. I resigned myself to spending another night on the recliner, then dozed off, slept fitfully until about six in the morning. I phoned Manning at nine just to check in.

"Yeah, Mr. Haskell, appreciate you checking in. Say, you wouldn't be acquainted with someone named Harold Benton, would you?"

"Harold Benton? No, it's not ringing a bell."

"He was shot sometime last night, knee-capped to be more specific. They picked him up about three blocks from Swirlee's house, if that helps jog your memory."

"No, it's not ringing any bells."

"Wanted on a half dozen felony charges, a couple of parole violations. He's back behind bars as we speak."

"Still not ringing any bells."

"Okay. Say, you wouldn't happen to know about a large amount of blood all over the rear patio at Swirlee's, would you?"

"I don't know anything about blood on the patio. The guy you mentioned, that could be the guy they called Benton. He assaulted me, assaulted Jill. They knee-capped him?" I asked.

"Looks that way, maybe. He's still in an uncooperative mood, but he'll have plenty of time to reflect, say eight to ten years, so we'll see. We recovered that duct tape from the hallway floor, I've already spoken to Miss Lydell. She's coming down for a hair and cell sample this morning. If we can match this tape to the Sneen murder I'd be a happy camper. Anything else you'd care to add?"

"No, Sir, just wishing you all the happiness."

"Good. Talk to you tomorrow."

"What'd he say?" Dog asked, dumping a third spoonful of sugar into his coffee.

"Harold Benton mean anything to you?"

"Should it?"

"He's the guy you knee-capped. They picked him up a few blocks away."

"Nice to put a name with it, but I don't think I ever heard of him. He made it a couple of blocks from Swirlee's? That's pretty good." He slurped more coffee.

"Blood on the patio?" I asked.

"They had some dumb-looking bastard standing out there. When I got him the stupid bastard was taking a piss in one of the flower gardens."

"Got him?"

"I left him on the patio, you know, so I could go inside, save your worthless ass, and Jill of course."

"Manning just mentioned a lot of blood, no body."

"He wasn't going anywhere, believe me."

I was drumming my fingers on the kitchen counter, thinking.

"Lola and Ponytail run away. Benton hobbles away. Do they stuff the body in the car?"

"Maybe. Sounds stupid, but they could have panicked. They had maybe sixty seconds tops to get out of there before the cops arrived. I don't know, that body will probably turn up somewhere. They always do. No sweat, nothing can tie us to it."

"So, if you're Lola and Ponytail, do you run? Stay? The cops are looking, so a credit card at a hotel might get you nailed. She doesn't strike me as the type to sleep in the back seat of a car anymore. But what if there's somewhere available? Some safe place where you could lay low?"

"What the hell are you talking about?"

"Maybe they went to Benton's, just to keep out of sight."

"Maybe."

"If only we knew where that was."

"Hey, you're the P.I. You're supposed to be able to figure all this shit out."

"Yeah, that's part of the problem, isn't it? Where's your computer?"

"Do I look like I have a computer?'

"Good point."

I phoned Sunnie Einer, my computer-wiz lady.

"Dev, long time no talk. Gee, let me guess, you're not calling to ask me out to dinner or the Guthrie or anything, but you need help with something?"

"See, that's why you make the big bucks, Sunnie, you're so smart."

"If I wanted to make big bucks I wouldn't stay in education. What's up?"

I explained my situation, sort of. I left out the part about the two or three murders, the threat on Jill's life, the threat on mine. As a matter of fact, I left out Jill all together. I skipped the part about taking the cash from the ice cream truck and just touched on Mr. Swirlee.

"No offense, but once again I feel like I'm not getting the complete story, Dev."

"See what I mean about being so smart?" I charmed.

"God, why don't you just Google this Benton person for starters?"

"Well, I'm sort of in a remote location and don't have a computer right now."

"Oh, God. No excuse...even *you* may have heard they have all these phones with apps now, call them smart phones. You could be sitting in your car somewhere and have access to all of this. Did you ever think of joining the twenty-first century and investing in an iPad or an iPhone?"

"I'm undercover right now," I said.

"Really? Doing what, pretending to be productive?"

"Sunnie, can you find out where this guy lives?"

"Oh, I suppose. Give me his name."

"Harold Benton," I said, then spelled the last name. "Look, I'll call you back..."

"Oh, please, for God's sake. Hold on, I've got it up now."

"Really?" I was genuinely surprised.

Sunnie ignored my remark.

"There's three of them in St. Paul, one is eighty-one, on Seminary Avenue, that's with the middle initial E. One is twenty-six, no middle initial, on Bragg Avenue. One is thirty-seven, middle initial J, on Ravoux Avenue. Any of those help?"

"Better give me all three again."

I wrote the addresses down, along with the phone numbers.

"We should get together, Dev, soon. I always feel so good about my life once I hear whatever nonsense you've been up to."

"Thanks, Sunnie. I'll give you a call when I've got this project wrapped up."

"She got you the info that fast?" Dog asked between coffee slurps.

"Yeah, computer shit. You want to come along and check these out, see if we can find our friends?"

Chapter Sixty-Seven

The first place we checked was Harold Benton, aged eighty-one, on Seminary Avenue. The Benton that had broken my nose, slapped Jill around, and Dog had kneecapped didn't strike me as a rose gardener or eighty-one. He could have been a son, but that just didn't seem likely.

The second Harold Benton, on Bragg Avenue, age twenty-six, came with a pretty, young wife and two toddlers on a swing set in the side yard. That didn't seem to work either.

The third Harold Benton, age thirty-seven, middle initial J, on Ravoux Avenue in Frogtown came with a house in need of paint and an overgrown lawn with dandelions. Neither of those facts was as convincing as Lola's black Mercedes parked almost, but not quite behind the house in the driveway.

"How 'bout we nail the doors shut, set the place on fire and then shoot them when they jump out the windows?" Dog was only half joking.

"Why don't we just call the cops?"

"I don't know about your ponytail pal, but there's a pretty good chance the woman can get lawyered up and released. How long you expect Jill to hide? Or, what if that bitch finds some other hot button, like going after your mom, or sister, or that computer chick? Or what if she's got some other goon running around? She can..."

"Okay, I get it. Any ideas?"

"I told you. We nail…"

"Come on."

"Yeah, as a matter of fact. I think it would be a lot easier if we got them out of the house. We call tonight, set up an exchange, disable the car, and when they come out we nail them. Pretty straightforward."

"Pretty cold."

"You've seen what they're like. You think this woman is gonna back off?"

"You're giving me another idea," I said.

"I don't want to hear we're going to convince her to turn herself in and confess for the good of society. That's going nowhere."

"No. Remember the warehouse deal. The guy goes out the window and lands on the sidewalk?"

"The one where you got two shots off? You mean the dead guy, Pinky Ackerman?"

"Think those folks might be interested to know where she is?"

"They just might be the ones putting pressure on her to come up with the money."

"Even better. Let's eliminate us as the middleman and just turn everything over to Pinky's family."

"It might work, but hold my idea as plan B, just in case."

Chapter Sixty-Eight

It took a number of phone calls, but eventually I was sitting in the office of Brendan Ackerman. Pinky's son.

"I'm still not clear why you contacted us," Brendan said.

There were three other guys in the office with us, and each outweighed me by about fifty pounds. They were clearly armed, and exhibited no sympathy for either Mr. Swirlee or Lola.

"It's like I told you. I've been to the police, they're investigating. Meanwhile, this woman kidnapped my girlfriend, assaulted both of us, and now she threatens to kill us if we don't give her money. Even if she's arrested, she'll probably get released once her lawyers are involved. At that point it really is in her best interest to kill both of us."

This seemed to be a perfectly normal course of business to two of the guys sitting on a couch, and they nodded slightly, understanding the logic of what I had just explained.

"And you want me to do what? Put a contract out on her like this is some sort of Hollywood movie?"

"No, Sir, I just want you to be aware of what I saw that afternoon. I want you to know I explained all this to the police. And, I want you to know what I, actually my girlfriend and I, have been going through as a result."

"And you think they're at this address?" He glanced at the address I'd written down.

"I'm pretty sure. The guy, Harold Benton, worked for her and Swirlee. Like I said, he did the nose job on me. Swirlee's car, a Mercedes 600, is parked in back. I saw it. I wrote the license number below the address there. Benton's already locked up." I didn't feel any pressing need to mention Benton had been kneecapped.

Brendan Ackerman stood and held out his hand.

"Mr. Haskell, I appreciate you calling and relaying this information. I think it would probably be in everyone's best interest if we let the authorities proceed and allow justice to take its course."

I shook his hand, looked him in the eye, and said, "My condolences to you and your family on your father's passing." Then I followed one of the heavies out of the office to a block of elevators where he left me.

I met Dog down at The Spot.

"So how'd it go?"

"I don't know. I guess I sort of expected him to slap me on the back and say thanks, we'll take it from here. Instead, he told me it would be best for the authorities to proceed and let justice take its course."

"He actually said that, the justice part?"

"Yep."

"You know, I just think it might be a good idea if a lot of people see you in a public place tonight."

"What?"

258

"Alibi."

"God, I just want this whole thing to be over."

Chapter Sixty-Nine

I couldn't tell you if it was the phone ringing or
my pounding headache caused by the phone ringing
that woke me up the next morning.

"Mr. Haskell, good afternoon."

I really wasn't in the mood for a cheerful
Detective Manning at the ungodly hour of, I checked,
almost two in the afternoon. I smacked some of the
Jameson off my teeth, then groaned,

"What?"

"I said good afternoon."

"Good afternoon," I grumbled.

"You know, you seem to be developing an
incredible knack of associating with people who fall
prey to violent deaths."

If something happened to Jill, I'd never forgive
myself.

"I'm not sure what or who you're talking about." I
swallowed down the lump in my throat.

"Reasonably attractive woman, she spent some
time with you just the other night...Lola Lentz."

Thank, God, I thought.

"Lola Len...you mean Swirlee's main squeeze?"

"Well, yes, and apparently his niece, among other things. Of course, I once again find myself suggesting it might be a good idea if you stopped by to chat. You do know where we're located?"

"Yeah, yeah, I think I can find the way," I said, struggling off the couch.

"Say about an hour from now?" Another police question that was not really a question.

"Sure, will I need a lawyer?"

"That's up to you," he said and hung up.

I made it down to the police station in an hour and fifteen minutes. Pretty good considering I had to shower, shave, dress, then spend twenty precious minutes looking for my car keys.

We were in my favorite sterile interview room. I sat across from Detective Manning, the grey Formica table scarred with brown, wormy looking cigarette burns between us.

"And you have chosen not to have counsel present at this time. Is that correct, Mr. Haskell?"

Manning was speaking into a recorder. He had just finished making me aware that we were being filmed as well.

"Please state for the record where you were last night between the hours of midnight and one-fifteen this morning."

"I was in The Spot bar, having several drinks with friends."

"And did you leave the premises at any time?"

"I did not."

"And do you have proof of this?"

"I do," I answered, then reached in my wallet and produced five receipts. I pushed them across the table toward Manning.

"Would you please state for the record what you have just given me."

"Those are five receipts from the ATM inside The Spot bar. They're a record of cash withdrawals from my checking account, each in the amount of twenty dollars, each marked with a date and a time. The first one is from about eleven-forty last night, then approximately every thirty minutes after that."

"Do you have any witnesses to the fact you remained at The Spot for the entire time?"

"Yes, the bartender, Jimmy. Then, of course, everyone I bought a drink for."

"And their names?"

"I only have first names, and some of that is a little foggy, but they're probably at The Spot right now, or they certainly will be later today."

For the next two to three hours Manning reviewed the questions he'd asked the day before. Eventually, the interview concluded.

"Do you have anything you wish to add, Mr. Haskell?"

"Only that I wish I had never been hired by Weldon Swirlmann, Mr. Swirlee, in the first place," I answered.

"Thank you, Mr. Haskell."

Aaron was waiting for us outside in the hallway.

"Mr. Haskell, thanks for your time. If you two will excuse me, I have a mountain of paperwork on this," Manning said, then walked away without another word.

Aaron watched him for a moment, then shook his head and without looking at me said, "You're buying dinner."

Chapter Seventy

Over dinner Aaron explained some things to me.

"Look, Manning has a really full plate. You can start with Bernie Sneen, then Mr. Swirlee. He's got Pinky Ackerman…"

"Who's that?" I asked.

He shot me a suspicious glance.

"Pinky Ackerman, a player, sort of like Tony Soprano only for real and a lot more vicious."

"Oh, that Pinky Ackerman."

"Yeah. So he gets tossed out a window and shot…"

"No kidding?"

He ignored me.

"Then there's three dead in some apparent ice cream truck robbery. We still can't get a handle on what that was about." Aaron eyed me for a long moment.

"The car accident with the ice cream truck?"

"Yeah, amazingly your buddy Swirlee, again. Then last night, this Lola broad and some other guy, in the house of a known associate."

I waited, but Aaron had stopped talking. A minute or two later he asked,

"Aren't you the least bit curious?"

"About what?"

"About what happened to her."

"Did you guys arrest her?"

"She was shot," Aaron said.

"How?"

He stared at me again for a long moment, clearly not sure.

"She was shot, along with some two-bit low life named Monty Norling. Looks like they may have been hiding out over in Frogtown, in some dive house. That Benton guy's as a matter of fact. Anyway, someone blocked the doors, then set the place on fire. Both of them were shot as they came out a window."

It was my turn to look unsure.

"Then someone seems to have calmly walked up and put another round right between their eyes."

"Professional?" I was still searching my foggy, drunken recollection of the previous night. Dog had been with me, I thought.

"Professional? No, whoever it was just got lucky. Yes, professional. Head shots look to have been fired from a distance of about six inches, pretty hard to miss at that range."

"Any suspects?"

"One, but he just eliminated himself with a stack of ATM receipts and a bar full of witnesses."

Chapter Seventy-One

I met Dog outside The Trend bar. It was the first time I'd seen him in almost a month.

When we stepped inside there was a noticeable drop in the conversational hum. Although there had been a statewide smoking ban for years, I immediately smelled cigarettes and maybe smoke from another source, completely illegal.

We walked to the back of the bar toward a neatly dressed black gentleman. This time he was wearing a dark green polo shirt, matching trousers, and highly polished shoes. The same expensive watch. He looked like a prosperous business man, just stirring a spoonful of sugar into his coffee as if waiting for his tee time.

"Thank you for seeing us, Walter," I said.

He gave a friendly nod and the conversational hum immediately rose four notches. He stared at my nose for a long moment.

"You look different, somehow," he said.

"No, it's still me."

"I don't mind telling you this has been one of my more unique transactions." He chuckled.

I palmed the roll of cash as we shook hands. Walter gave us the usual directions to our new vehicles.

"I don't know, man," Dog said, shaking his head as we crossed the street to the Rainbow Food parking lot.

"What?"

"Well, let's just say you've done some pretty stupid things in your life, but this has to be up there, maybe the top one or two. It just ain't necessary."

"I think it's the least I can do."

"Seems pretty goddamn extreme to me, but what do I know?"

"Exactly. Besides, I feel like I owe it for some reason."

The keys were under the floor mats, just like before. We started the two vehicles, Dog signaled with a thumbs up and then followed when I drove off. Not that I'd want to do it for a living, but it was a fun fifteen-minute drive, racing through the streets and across the High Bridge.

We swung onto Ohio Street. The contractor's trailer was parked in front of the Giant Scoop Office. We pulled into the parking bay. I honked the horn, and Dog rang the bell on his truck a couple of times.

Jill stepped out of the office area. She was splattered with paint and held a roller in her hand.

"What in the hell is this?" she asked wide eyed.

"Little something to help you get restarted," I said.

"But...but...where? God, they look brand new. I...I...holy shit!" she said, walking around the two ice cream trucks.

Fortunately Walter's team had painted over the pink and blue Mr. Swirlee logos, removed the Swirlee hood ornament and switched over the dreadful "Little

266

Dog Gone" chime to a simple bell sound, then installed new coolers and the twelve treats menu on the back.

"I really don't know what to tell you. Except, oh God. I've been such a…"

"Don't," I said.

Chapter Seventy-Two

We were sitting at my kitchen counter, sipping chilled, cheap white wine. Heidi and me.

"You know, in a weird way having the head cut off sort of improves the look of that fish. Now if you'd just take it down all together, it would really spruce the place up."

"Yeah, whatever."

"Oh for God's sake. Dev, get over her. Look, you've been moping around for the last couple of weeks and everyone has…"

"Well, I mean, maybe just a phone call or something."

"Look, what can she say? You gave her two ice cream trucks for God's sake. I mean, you barely know her, right? If you're really being honest."

"You know, I've been asking myself to do that a lot lately, be honest."

"Will you stop it? Look, you've been an absolute downer for weeks now."

"You think my idea for breast milk ice cream might have put her off?" I asked.

"Look, I can't take this. When the pity party is over give me a call. But it's not much fun seeing you like this. I better get going anyway. I got a hell of a day tomorrow."

"Thanks for stopping."

As a mark of my depression, I left the wine unfinished, wandered out to my living room, stretched on the couch and dozed off.

The ringing bell woke me. A bright yellow ice cream truck was parked in front of my house. Jill was just climbing out. She saw me looking out the window, waved, gave a big smile, then held up two bottles of white wine.

The End

If you enjoyed Dev's adventures in <u>Mr. Swirlee</u>, check out his antics in the sample of <u>Bite Me</u> just after my shameless self promotion.

Help yourself to these stand alone titles.

They're all available on Amazon.

Baby Grand
Chow For Now
Slow, Slow, Quick, Quick
Merlot
Finders Keepers
End of the Line

Irish Dukes (Fight Card Series)
written under the pseudonym Jack
Tunney

The following titles comprise the Dev Haskell series;
Russian Roulette: (1)
Mr. Swirlee: (2)
Bite Me: (3)
Bombshell: (4)
Tutti Frutti: (5)
Last Shot: (6)
Ting-A-Ling: (7)
Crickett: (8)
Bulldog: (9)
Double Trouble (10)
Twinkle Toes
(A free Dev Haskell short story)

Email: mikefaricyauthor@gmail.com
Facebook: Mike Faricy Books
Facebook: Dev Haskell
Twitter: @mikefaricybooks

Here's a free sample of <u>Bite Me</u>, happy reading.

Bite Me

<u>Chapter One</u>

It was bigger than a steak knife, not quite a carving blade, but still capable of doing some very serious damage. The knife came with a bright red handle, the kind sculpted to fit your fingers and hold a blade that gleamed viciously. I dodged the swipes again and pleaded.

"Put the knife down. Just put the knife down, please." I tried to sound calm.

Another wild swipe, this one slashing very close to the tip of my nose.

"Look, can we talk about this? Take it easy." I was aware panic had caused my voice to raise about two more notches. I was hoping I didn't have to throw a punch.

"Get out. Just get out. I want you out of here now, do you hear me? Now! Get out," she screamed.

"Okay, okay, Christ just let me get dressed and…"

"Get out now or I swear I'll cut you up into the tiniest little pieces. I will, you creep. I swear I will."

"Hey, Kiki, I believe you, okay? Just let me get my jeans on. If you could just hand them to me and…"

"Get out of my bedroom," she screamed, then slashed wildly again through the air.

"Just give me my jeans. I promise I'll leave, but I have to have some clothes. Look, you can keep the shirt. I never liked that one anyway and…"

"Get out, get out, get out," she screamed, slashing back and forth with every shriek.

Talk about a date going down the drain. Everything was fine until the shots of tequila, mores the pity. Still, I thought there might be an outside chance she was just playing hard to get.

"Look, maybe if we just got back into bed …"

She lunged at me, tripped over my jeans on the floor and fell. She curled up in a fetal position, naked on her bedroom carpet and began to sob. Even when she was trying to kill me she looked incredibly hot. I couldn't stop staring at her thick brunette hair, creamy white skin, fantastic hips and those cute little feet.

"Sorry, sorry, I'm just such a bitch, well sometimes," she sobbed.

No argument there, but the only person I was feeling sorry for right now was me. I picked up the knife, quickly pulled on my jeans, then slipped on my shoes.

"Keep the boxers and socks, Kiki. It's been a unique experience. I've never spent the night with a woman who kept a knife under her pillow."

I pulled the shirt over my head then buckled my belt as I made for the bedroom door.

"Phone me tomorrow, Dev, promise?" she called, sitting up and wiping the tears from her eyes. Her smeared mascara looked like hastily applied war paint.

"Yeah, sure," I lied hoping she would just stay put so I could make it to the front door.

"I'll lock up behind you," she called, then staggered to her feet and hurried to catch up, sniffling as she came. She stopped at the dining room table, poured herself a quick shot and tossed it back. "Ahhh." She grabbed an apple from a dish in the center of the dinning room table and continued toward the front door.

I realized I was still carrying the knife and increased my pace without actually running. I made it to the door and opened it just as she hurried across the living room.

"Do you have to go? You'll call?" she asked, standing naked in the doorway. She calmly took a bite out of the apple and waited for my reply.

The only call I was going to make was to 911, but then, why bother? One look at Kiki, gorgeous, naked, asking me to stay and the cops would haul me away.

"Hey, I've got an early meeting. Catch you later." I said and then pulled the door closed behind me. She snapped the lock on the other side. I paused, left the knife on the porch and wondered what time it was. The sun was up, birds were chirping. My watch was still inside, probably somewhere in Kiki's bedroom. Screw it. I could always get another watch.

"Bastard!" I heard her scream inside the house. Then, the unmistakable sound of something shattering as the shot glass sailed through a pane in the side window.

That was my traveling music. I climbed behind the wheel of my DeVille and raced off. The clock on my dash read three-twenty-seven, but it had been like that for the better part of the year. I started pushing radio buttons to see if someone might mention the time. They didn't.

Once home I pushed a chair in front of the door just in case Kiki showed up to make good on her promise to kill me. I napped fitfully on the couch until I finally gave up and drifted over to my office. Not that

I had anything to do here, except look out the window at The Spot bar across the street. It was too late to join the lunchtime crowd and too early to stop in for a nightcap.

I got six months office rent free in lieu of payment on a case I'd worked last New Years. A guy I knew bought a bar, hired a number of employees based on breast size, then wondered why he was losing money. Three nights of me posing as a new hire got the answers to most of his questions. If he ran the building where my office was anything like his bar, he wasn't going to stay in business very long.

I'd been staring out my second story office window for fifteen or twenty minutes, leering at female passersby when the phone rang.

"Haskell Investigations."

"Mr. Haskell, please," a male voice said, then coughed.

"You got him."

"Oh, well, this is Farrell J. Earley. I got your name from my sister, Kiki."

"Kiki?"

"Yes, I spoke with her about an hour ago."

"Yeah, well, look, I can explain. See your sister…"

"Relax, I know, she can kinda go over the edge every now and again."

"That's an understatement. It would have been nice to know that before she had a knife in her hand. She threatened to cut me up into tiny pieces."

"That's my Kiki."

"Well, look, I don't know what she told you, but I can assure you that I behaved like a perfect gentleman."

"Yeah, sure you did. That's her hot button, gentlemen. To tell you the truth, Mr. Haskell, I don't really care. Thing is, while Kiki was ranting and screaming she mentioned that you were a private investigator. I'd like to hire you."

"Call me Dev," I said.

"Okay, Dev. I'd like to contract your services. That is, if you're available."

About the only thing I had going on was Jameson night at The Spot on Thursday.

"Well, why don't we meet, discuss your needs and then if you're still interested I'll see if I can adjust my schedule."

"Can you make it today?"

"I can. Where would you like to meet?"

"I'm over here at Craze, K-R-A-Z," he pronounced each letter like it would mean something to me, it didn't. I hadn't the foggiest idea what in the hell he was talking about.

"That still in the same place?" I asked, hoping for a clue.

"Yep."

"I'm in a meeting until about four, rush hour and all. What would be the quickest way over there from downtown?"

"You know with the construction and all, take I-94, get off at Snelling."

"That's what I figured. Pretty sure I know the building, but give me the address anyway," I said, thinking come on, man.

"Fifteen thirty-seven, we're up on the sixth floor."

It was like pulling teeth to find out where in the hell he was.

"Mr. Earley, give me your phone number there in case I'm running late I don't anticipate any problems, but better safe than sorry."

He gave me his number. I hung up, then dialed the number, figuring the receptionist would tell me the street.

Someone answered with a cough, Farrell again, apparently his cell phone.

"Hello?"

"Mr. Earley? Dev Haskell again. I must have misdialed, in the process of adjusting my schedule. Sorry to bother you."

"Not a bother. Still see you at four?"

"Four it is."

Chapter Two

It turned out KRAZ was a radio station. Who knew? Probably not too many people based on the tiny office and even smaller broadcast booth. The first three floors in the grimy building served as a warehouse for the Abbott Paint Company. The halls were a version of government grey, the stairs worn, poured concrete. What sounded like a printing press was clunking away up on the sixth floor and far down the hall. Most of the small office suites appeared to be vacant.

A walnut stained door led into the corner suite. There was a handwritten sign in black marker crookedly taped above the mail slot, 'KRAZ National Headquarters'. I opened the door and walked in, or at least I tried. About three quarters into opening the door, it struck the edge of a desk forcing me to make a quick side step.

"Hello," I called still holding the door open.

The desk, a mid 60's surplus model, was covered with stacks of files. Random scrawled notes were taped to the wall behind the desk. Aging newspapers and advertising circulars littered the stacks of files and spilled onto the floor.

"Hello, anyone home?" I called again.

I heard a raspy cough followed by the appearance of a guy in the doorway off to the right. He wore large, dark framed glasses, wrinkled, cream-colored cotton slacks and a grey t-shirt that read "KRAZ, America's Right!" in bright red letters. He held a cigarette with a two-inch ash in his right hand.

"Hi, I'm looking for Farrell Earley," I said.

He took a drag, thought about that for a moment, then asked, "Do you have an appointment?"

"Yeah, Devlin Haskell. He's expecting me." I would have handed the guy my card, but I'd run out a few weeks back.

He exhaled a blue cloud then gave a slight cough.

"Oh yeah. Haskell nice to meet you. Farrell J. Earley. Any problem finding the place?" he asked, extending his hand. He looked nothing like his gorgeous, knife wielding crazy sister.

"No, no problem, exactly where I thought you were," I lied.

"Come on back to the office I want you to meet Tommy. Give you an idea of what we're dealing with, see what you think." He was saying this as we walked through what must have been an office at one time. The room was crammed with stacks of blue and red plastic crates filled with cords, key boards, three or four antique computer monitors. The things probably leaked radiation and looked as old as me.

"Pardon the mess, we're in the process of updating," he said making for a door on the far wall.

Through the door we entered a dusty office with walls painted a baby-shit brown color. A red-faced guy with a crew cut sat behind the desk, typing on an electric typewriter.

"With you in a moment," he said, not looking up, fingers dancing across the typewriter keys. With every key stroke a ball about the size of a golf ball struck the paper.

Farrell motioned me toward a dusty, black leather couch. We sat there and waited in a blue cloud of his cigarette smoke. Eventually the typing was complete and the guy pulled the sheet from the typewriter, then placed it face down on a stack of paper, turned in his chair and looked from me to Farrell, then back to me.

"Sorry about that, can never be too careful. Tomorrow's broadcast, do that on the computer and there's no telling who'll get hold of it and use it for their own degenerate purposes. All right then, who do we have here?"

"This is the fella I was telling you about. The private investigator, Dennis Haskell."

"Devlin, Devlin Haskell," I corrected.

"Thompson Barkwell," he said, holding out his hand.

I had to get up off the couch and take two steps to grab it. He gave me a limp shake for the effort.

"Nice to meet you, Mr. Barkwell."

"Please, call me Thompson. We get to know one another better and you can call me Tommy. But, let's keep it at Thompson for right now, shall we?"

'Fine with me, jerk.' I thought, smiled and nodded. "Yes sir, I look forward to getting to know you much better."

"Farrell bring you up to speed with our situation?"

"Not really. What seems to be the problem?"

They looked back and forth for a long moment. Eventually Thompson took a deep breath, leaned back in his chair and said, "Here at K-R-A-Z we like to think of ourselves as the voice of the American future. A right thinking America. We…"

The future of America is the electric typewriter? I was wondering why I should even be surprised. After all, they got my name from that knife-wielding lunatic, Kiki. I wondered if she'd calmed down yet. Then I remembered her breasts bouncing up and down while she swung the knife at me. Wondered if maybe it had just been a one time sort of melt down and maybe we could …

"… view us as a threat to their socialistic ways, and therefore intend to deal with us accordingly."

They sat and looked at me, waiting for a reaction. I tried to erase Kiki from my mind.

"So what do you think?" Thompson finally said.

"Give me that last part again."

"Not much to it. The note said that we were a threat to their socialistic ways and therefore they intended to deal with us accordingly."

"So many questions," I said, stalling for time.

"Would you care to share them?" Thompson asked.

"Well, first off, tell me about the note. How did it come to you? Where is it now? Did you inform the police?"

"Like I said, it was shoved under the door when we arrived yesterday. Yes, we did call the police," Thompson said.

"They've got the note now," Farrell added.

"I see, I see," I said, hoping to sound like I did.

"Of course, they're probably worried about equal rights and the other nonsense that's become the left's mantra. While patriots like us just soldier on, moving forward, constantly under fire," Thompson said.

"So you consider this a legitimate threat, the note? You don't think someone might just be pulling your leg?"

"Pulling our leg? You've got to be kidding. No, we've struck a nerve, probably more than one. No doubt you've listened to our broadcasts. You know how they are."

"To tell you the truth I don't listen as often as I'd like to."

"Which was your favorite?" Thompson asked.

Farrell exhaled another blue cloud and leaned forward on the couch.

"Oh, it would be tough to pick just one." I dodged.

"But, you must have a favorite."

"I really like them all. No, no, too tough to narrow it down to just one. Honest."

"I know what you mean," Thompson said, looking thoughtful.

Farrell nodded and fired up another cigarette using the butt of his last one.

"Okay, so we're working with what? A death threat?" I asked.

"Exactly," replied Thompson.

"Yeah, death threat, definitely a death threat," Farrell chimed in.

"And what exactly would you like me to do?"

"Well, first and foremost, protection, that's paramount. Something happens to either one of us and the movement dies, right here, right now." Thompson struck the desk top four times with his index finger in perfect time to *'right here, right now'*.

"Then, when you're not protecting, we'd like you to get to the bottom of this. Find out what sort of pinko, commy group of misfits uses murder and intimidation as a logical consequence of open dialogue."

"What about the police?" I asked.

"Can't be trusted," Farrell said.

Thompson nodded his head in agreement.

"What sort of protection do you want?" I asked.

"You carry a gun, don't you?"

"Yeah, I'm licensed."

"For the love of… hell, we're all licensed, if that's what you want to call it. Part of our second amendment rights. But we need some extra firepower. These folks will stop at nothing."

"Look, no offense, but so far all you've got is a note slipped under the door. You've given that to the police. They'll check it out for you. From what you tell me it sounds like it could be as simple as a college prank."

"A college prank? You can't honestly believe that threat represents a college prank. Although, given the state of what passes for education now-a-days…" Thompson seemed to drift off somewhere distant then slapped the top of his desk. "No, I'm afraid we don't have the luxury of living in such a cavalier fashion, Mr. Haskin."

"Haskell, Devlin Haskell," I reminded, smiling.

"We're the last line of defense before the damn train goes off the rails."

"Meaning?" I was beginning to think Thompson was a legend in his own mind.

"Meaning we've hit a nerve, sir. They know we speak the truth and they can't stand that - the truth."

'In for a penny, in for a pound' I thought.

"So you'd like protection, here, at your office?"

"Our station, and yes, here, while we broadcast," Thompson said.

"It's when we're the most vulnerable, when we're on the air." Farrell added.

"Like I said before, I haven't been able to listen as often as I would like, remind me what your hours are," I said.

"We're on from ten to ten-fifteen in the morning, noon to twelve-fifteen, three to three-fifteen and then the drive home hour, five-thirty to five-forty-five." Thompson squeaked back in his office chair and looked like he just won the lottery.

"We tape our message the day before, then play it four times the following day," Farrell said as he exhaled another long blue cloud.

"It's a well-known fact people have to hear something four times within twenty-four hours before they begin to pick it up," Thompson expounded.

"You guys have any sponsors?" I asked.

They looked back and forth from one another again. Eventually Thompson said, "I really don't feel comfortable divulging that information at this time. Suffice to say we do have sponsors and are enlisting more everyday."

'I'll take that as a no,' I thought.

"When would you like me to start?"

"The sooner, the better," Thompson said and looked at his watch.

"It's time I got into the sound booth," Farrell said, gave a raspy cough and then followed it with a long drag on his cigarette burning it down to his nicotine-stained fingers.

"Does a nine forty-five start suit you?" Thompson asked.

"I can do that. I'd better get going, I've got some schedules to shuffle around. I'll see the two of you here, tomorrow, nine forty-five."

"You're just what we need." Thompson smiled, and held out his hand for another limp, dead-fish shake.

As I followed Farrell out I heard the electric typewriter start up again. We walked past the plastic crates of obsolete equipment. Out in the front office or whatever they called it, Farrell said, "Appreciate you taking our case on, Mr. Haskin. We'll all sleep a little better tonight knowing you're on the job."

"Haskell, H-a-s-k-e-l-l," I spelled it for him.

"Right." He half chuckled.

"I'll be here at nine forty-five tomorrow. Just keep a close eye out on your way home tonight and back in tomorrow. Let's have you guys keep a low profile until we get things sorted out, okay?"

"That won't be a problem."

"See you tomorrow," I said and left.

Chapter Three

I was buying another round at The Spot. I'd been buying all night. I was beyond the point of caring and was holding court on a bar stool dangerously close to two drunks throwing darts.

"One of your deadbeat clients finally pay up?" Jimmy asked as he filled the glasses with the next round.

"Even better, I got a job where I don't have to work." I laughed.

"So what's new 'bout that."

"No, I mean, I just have to sit around. Someone pulled a joke on these clowns and they bought it. Hired me for protection," I said, then washed that down with a healthy couple of swallows.

"You for protection, that is a joke." Jimmy laughed.

"Yeah? Well, you ever hear of a radio station called craze?"

"Craze… you mean like nuts? What is that some weird punk rock, kid thing?"

"No, K-R-A-Z, supposed to be something right with America deal or, I don't know. I'll take another, Jimmy," I said and drained my glass.

"You driving?"

"Yeah, but not all that far, so relax."

Over the course of the evening I asked around. No one in the bar had ever heard of KRAZ. The next thing I knew it was closing time, Jimmy locked the door, let me finish my beer, but wouldn't give me another. I apparently made it home all right because I woke up on my couch at about six-thirty the following morning. I stumbled to the kitchen, put some coffee on and curled back up on the couch. When I next looked at the clock on my microwave it was nine twenty.

I threw a semi-clean shirt on, gobbled some mints, raced out the door and over to KRAZ.

Farrell was sucking the last inch of life from his current cigarette when I bounced the office door off the front desk. I was still a little breathless and red in the face from rushing to make it modestly late.

"You guys ought to move that thing," I said, nodding at the front desk.

He exhaled, sipped from his coffee mug and smiled, but didn't say anything.

I saw Thompson through the doorway. He was standing next to the stacks of red and blue crates. It was the first time I'd seen him standing. At least I thought he was standing. I put him at about five foot three, on a good day.

He glanced at his watch, raised an eyebrow then shook his head.

"I believe our agreement was nine-forty-five," he called.

"It was. I got here early, strolled around the building and the parking lots checking some things, making myself familiar with the area. Nice to know what I'm dealing with. First line of defense is out there, not in here." I had to admit that sounded so good, even I half believed it.

Farrell looked surprised. Thompson looked like he wasn't sure. I seized the opportunity.

"Anything seem out of the ordinary? Another note, a phone call, someone following either of you, noise out in the hallway?"

They both shook their heads.

"Okay, you're on the air shortly?"

"Twelve minutes," Farrell said and lit up another cigarette.

"Mind if I watch?"

"Be my guest." He exhaled.

By this time Thompson had returned to his lair.

Eleven minutes later I was standing behind Farrell in a converted closet. We had to hunch over because of the shelf that ran across the top. There was a bare light bulb in the ceiling with a string attached to turn it off and on. Fortunately, someone had the foresight to remove the pole and clothes hangers.

Farrell wore a set of headphones. He was seated at a tiny desk at one end of the closet with a laptop in front of him. The dusty screen on the laptop displayed a digital readout ticking down the minutes before broadcast and then the last sixty seconds. The final ten seconds clicked past furiously in increments of a tenth of a second. With three seconds left, Farrell slowly, deliberately raised his index finger and pushed the enter key on the laptop. Then he leaned back and listened for a moment before he removed his headphones.

"There you go, we're on the air," he said and pushed back his chair.

Still hunched over I had to back up to exit the closet. Farrell took a final drag, then fired up a fresh cancer stick and backed out.

"We record the *word*, as we like to call it, the night before. Then upload it and we're set to go. We could set the download for any time, but I like to do the manual play. Gets me into the groove if you know what I mean."

Actually I didn't. Somehow Farrell 'in the groove' didn't seem to compute.

"So that's it until noon?"

"Well, we stand by, answer the phones, sign up volunteers, get people organized… that sort of thing."

"Oh, so listeners call?"

"Well, they could. I mean that's what we're hoping will happen, sometime, anyway."

It didn't happen.

The routine was the same at noon, three and five-thirty, only even more boring. I walked around the building and the parking lot a few times just to stay awake. At six I drifted into Thompson's office. He was pounding away on the future of America, his electric typewriter.

"You feel comfortable with me leaving for the day?"

He stopped hammering the typewriter keys, squeaked his chair around and nodded with a determined look across his face.

"I'd say we sent out a pretty strong message today."

"Your broadcast?"

"Broadcast? No, you, our protection. We won't be silenced. Matter of fact it's provided me inspiration, freedom of speech," he said and patted the one-inch stack of paper on the desk. Just like yesterday it was face down.

"Tomorrow's broadcast?" I asked.

"Exactly."

"Farrell reads that for fifteen minutes and then you play it four times a day?"

"We do."

"Ever think of maybe shortening it? I don't know, cutting it down to maybe fifteen or twenty seconds? Maybe play some music or something?"

"We've done that from time to time, or a version. We've had 'America The Beautiful' as a background accompaniment once in a while, some Sousa marches."

"Yeah, I was thinking more like just music, maybe something popular, current, get your audience interested and..."

"Some drug culture thing? That it? You've been in the gutter too long, Haskell. We're not trying to be popular, if that's what your angle is. We're here to tell the truth, something that often times is unpopular." He placed some added emphasis to the *un* in unpopular.

"Well, I kind of like the gutter, to tell you the truth. But, I was thinking fifteen minutes is an awfully long time to listen to someone going on and on."

"On and on, that's what you think we do?"

"You know what I mean. I just wonder if you aren't missing your mark a bit by trying to tell them too many things. You know the KISS acronym, Keep It Simple Stupid."

"No, I guess I missed that one," he said and squeaked around to face his typewriter, signaling the end of our conversation.

"Well, I don't want to piss you off, but whatever you ran as your message didn't seem to cut it. You played the thing four separate times. Fifteen minutes a crack, that's an hour and unless you got a call center tucked away somewhere, I never heard a phone ring all day long, ever. Not trying to tell you how to run your business, Thompson, that's just my opinion."

"That's part of what's gone wrong with this great nation. Everything comes down to the ten-second sound bite. Is that what freedom means to you, ten seconds?"

I waited for a moment, a long moment, maybe ten seconds worth.

"Nine forty-five tomorrow, right?"

Chapter Four

It was more of the same the next day. The term boring wouldn't begin to do it justice. Add to that the hot, humid weather and a nap had become one of my top priorities.

Immediately after the dreadful afternoon broadcast Thompson and Farrell had me follow them out of the office to the stairway. As we trudged down the six flights of stairs they filled me in on their latest brain fart. Then Thompson said, "So we up and decided, let's just advance in another direction."

"Do you think this is a good idea? I mean, wasn't the plan that you were going to keep a low profile?" I asked.

"Within reason, but one can never be timid when freedom is involved," Thompson replied. He sounded breathless and he still had another flight to waddle down.

"But a press conference in front of the building?" I said, "I don't know, it…"

"That's right, you don't know. We'll be just in time to hit the Six O'clock news. Look, Haskin, I'll handle the PR, you just handle protection," Thompson wheezed, then pushed the door open and we stepped outside.

There were two cameramen and two people I guessed to be reporters standing there. They were chatting, waiting and looking very bored. One guy flicked a cigarette off to the side as the door closed behind us. I had news for them. It was about to get a lot worse. A woman I sort of recognized in a blonde way was on her cell phone with her back to us.

"Ladies and gentlemen, thank you for coming. I'm Thompson Barkwell, CEO of K-R-A-Z, craze radio, seven-forty on your dial. I'm sure you're all familiar with our on air personality, Farrell J. Earley."

Farrell nodded, pushed his glasses back up on his nose and exhaled a blue cloud of smoke. Thompson continued, "We're here today to discuss an extremely serious situation. Over the course of the past seventy-two hours we…"

"Excuse me, please. Please, excuse me, sir, Mr. Barky, is it?" asked the blonde on the cell phone.

"Barkwell, Thompson Barkwell."

"Sure, Tiffany Kinny, from *The Source*. Would you mind starting over? Sorry. I was on the phone to one of my kids and by the way, do you have a hand out?"

"A hand out, no. I do not have a hand out. Maybe you could listen. I have some prepared remarks, and then I'll take your questions." Thompson suddenly produced a sheaf of papers that looked like a small phone book. He cleared his throat and began reading.

"It is time that the concept of Freedom of Speech in this great nation is taken back by the people. The very patriots who, in 1776, refused to stand idly by while…"

One of the camera men lowered his camera, shrugged and looked very bored. I'd have said Tiffany what's-her-face stopped writing, but then I was pretty sure she had never started. Thompson droned on, and on. Farrell had assumed a sort of military parade rest position and stared straight ahead wearing a more dazed look than usual. I tuned the whole thing out and watched a bus fifty yards away at the corner.

By now Thompson was working his way through the Gettysburg address.

"… it is for us the living rather, to be dedicated here to the unfinished work…"

He lunged, or did he fall? I didn't know. I was just coming back to reality when I heard the shot, and then another. I saw the car race down the street. Farrell was over Thompson, shielding him. I glanced down the street, but couldn't read the license plate. Hell, I couldn't even tell if the plate was from Minnesota. A nondescript grey or silver something, but I couldn't catch the make of the car.

One thing for sure, the cameras were suddenly rolling, focused on Thompson and Farrell. Thompson mumbled something to Farrell, they got up together, and dusted themselves off.

"Is everyone all right? Anyone hurt?"

"Jesus Christ, did you get that shit?" Tiffany Kinny asked a cameraman from where she was crouched behind a trash can.

"Anything Haskell?" Farrell asked.

I shook my head, still staring down the street. The car was long gone.

"Nothing, not a thing."

"Folks, who knew? They think they can silence the craze, K-R-A-Z, seven-forty on your dial. Seven-forty, get it? Seven four, like July fourth. Seventh month, fourth day. Freedom, Freedom, we will not be silenced. We've hit a nerve, people. We're speaking the truth and the lefties don't like it. No, sir, we will not be silenced."

The cameras continued to roll as Thompson spoke. Tiffany shook her hair left and right, then lunged into camera range moving closer to Thompson.

"Who is this gentleman?" she asked Thompson, indicating me with a movement of her head.

"Security. It's the sad state of affairs in our great nation that we have to hire protection in order to speak the truth. The silent majority can not continue to sit idly by while…"

I was wondering where the rounds hit. They should have hit the building, or the steps or someone. Nothing. I heard a distant siren that seemed to be getting closer.

Thanks for sampling. Dev's about to step in it, again. Pick up a copy of **<u>Bite Me</u>** for all the details and check out my other titles on Amazon, all the best, happy reading and thanks, Mike Faricy.

Made in the USA
San Bernardino, CA
23 February 2018